"Magnolia McCabe. Are you accusing me of just wanting to spend time with you?"

Maggie flushed at Hart's low, flirtatious tone.

His smile widening, and with his son cradled tenderly against his chest, he inched closer. Maggie rocked back in her chair and tried to calm the immediate spark of excitement she felt. And instead got sucked in by his gaze. It took every ounce of self-control she had not to rise and join them both.

"Because it's really not true," Hart teased gently. He sat on the edge of her desk, facing her. "It's Henry here who is completely and utterly crushing on you." He rubbed the toddler's back. "Henry, whose heart you seem to have captured."

It was easy to see the staggering resemblance between Hart and his son. Both were incredibly handsome and engaging in their own way.

Maggie felt something catch in her heart.

Runaway
Lone Star Bride

CATHY GILLEN
THACKER

MILLS & BOON®

First published in Great Britain 2014
by Mills & Boon, an imprint of Harlequin (UK) Limited,
Large Print edition 2014
Eton House, 18-24 Paradise Road,
Richmond, Surrey, TW9 1SR

© 2014 Cathy Gillen Thacker

ISBN: 978-0-263-23935-5

CATHY GILLEN THACKER

is married and a mother of three. She and her husband spent eighteen years in Texas and now reside in North Carolina. Her mysteries, romantic comedies and heartwarming family stories have made numerous appearances on bestseller lists, but her best reward, she says, is knowing one of her books made someone's day a little brighter. A popular Mills & Boon author for many years, she loves telling passionate stories with happy endings, and thinks nothing beats a good romance and a hot cup of tea! You can visit Cathy's website, www.cathygillenthacker.com, for more information on her upcoming and previously published books, recipes and a list of her favorite things.

Daisy, darling, this one's for you.

Chapter One

One look at her lovely face, and Hart Sanders knew. Magnolia McCabe was going to run.

It didn't matter that Maggie's fiancé, plus her twin sister and her groom, and all their families, had taken the coveted Wedding Train to the very top of Sanders Mountain and were now standing in Nature's Cathedral.

Nor was it important that the minister had gotten halfway through the ceremony that would join Maggie and her intended husband forevermore.

The only thing that mattered to Maggie in that instant was how *trapped* she felt.

And Hart knew from his years of military training that cornered people did one of two things.

They either cowered and froze. Or said to heck with the consequences and bolted for freedom. His gut told him that the beautiful brunette was about to choose the latter option.

As if on cue, Maggie McCabe shoved her bouquet at her maid of honor and picked up the hem of her wedding gown. She revealed a pair of fancy white cowgirl boots that sure seemed to be made for running as she dashed past the four hundred startled guests and made her way toward the thick woods surrounding them.

A collective gasp echoed through the flower-strewn clearing. "Maggie!" her fiancé, Gus Radcliffe, yelled as the white-satin-and-lace-clad bride disappeared into the cover of green. "What the—?" "Go after her!" another guest shouted hysterically.

Not about to see one calamity turn into two,

Hart stepped forward and lifted a staying hand. "Everyone, stay put! The last thing we need is anyone getting lost in the woods." He looked out into the crowd reassuringly. "I'll find her and escort her to safety."

Hart turned to Maggie's twin sister, Callie McCabe, feeling a little sorry for her. This was her wedding, too, that her sister had just disrupted. "If you want to get married today while there is still daylight, you better go on with your part of the double-wedding ceremony," he advised, kindly.

Callie appeared to waver.

Her parents, Drs. Jackson and Lacey McCabe, seemed to understand the wisdom of limiting the damages as best they could. Jackson leaned down to whisper something in his remaining daughter's ear.

Realizing enough time had been wasted, Hart left the rest of them to sort it out, and followed the runaway bride's path.

MAGGIE COULDN'T BELIEVE IT. She'd barely been gone five minutes and she was already completely lost. Knowing, however, if she stayed where she was and tried to get her bearings, someone would likely come after her, she kept right on plowing through the heavy cover of cedar, oak and pine trees.

The old logging road she'd seen from the train had to be here somewhere, Maggie reassured herself. All she had to do was find it, and—

Caught up short, Maggie bit down on an oath. The hem of her long skirt had snagged on the branches of a thick, thorny bush. Hurriedly, she tried to work it free and stabbed her fingertips in the process. "Ouch!" She pressed the bleeding appendages to her mouth, and when that did almost nothing to abate the sharp pain, another string of very unladylike words escaped her lips.

"Nice."

At the sound of the deep male voice, she

swore again. Louder and more virulently this time. And was rewarded with a chuckle.

"Need some help there?"

Maggie dropped her still-stinging hand, drew a breath and turned.

Of course it was him. Hart Sanders. The just-out-of-the-military son and heir to the Double Knot Wedding Ranch. Temporarily at loose ends, he'd been tapped—unwillingly, it seemed— into service as the official escort for the McCabe double wedding. She had noticed him in the foreground at the rehearsal dinner the evening before. And yet, disinterested as he had appeared to be in the festivities, he could not seem to stop looking at her. Or, if she were honest, she at him.

Embarrassed color heating her face, Maggie lifted her chin. This crazy attraction she seemed to be having for Hart Sanders was nothing but a symptom of the inadvisability of her marriage plans. A symptom she desperately needed to ignore.

Aware he was the only thing between her and escape, she retorted, "No. I do not need any help." She made a shooing motion. "So you can go on about your business."

He smiled grimly. "Hate to break it to you, but at the moment you *are* my business."

Maggie glared. "Like heck I am! I got myself into this mess, and I can darn well get myself out."

"Well, this will be fun." He folded his arms in front of him. Waited.

Determined to do this on her own, she knelt down and gave another, less delicate, tug. This time, to her satisfaction, her skirt did come free of the thorn bush. It also ripped from shin to midthigh, revealing way too much stocking-clad leg, as well as her silk magnolia blossom-studded garter. Although at this point, Maggie thought wearily, what did that matter?

Aware that Hart was still watching her intently, she lifted her skirt in her hands and continued on her way, stumbling along on the uneven ground.

He said nothing more.

Surprised, she turned and found he had been following her. Soundlessly. Effortlessly. To the point they were now just a mere two feet from each other.

She stared up at the six-foot-four Texan, born and bred. He was solid muscle. Combat ready. And gorgeous, head-to-toe, from the top of his short light brown hair and deep sable eyes. She stared at his square jaw and the ruggedly masculine planes of his face, wishing he weren't so damned confident.

"I said," she repeated, wearily, "that I did not need your help!"

Hart nodded sagely, about as movable as a two ton boulder. "I heard you."

Apparently, he just hadn't believed her.

She swallowed as he stepped even closer, feeling the heat radiating from his body. She drew in another breath, taking in the scent of him, so utterly crisp and male. Like the men in the wedding party, he was wearing a tuxedo and white shirt. Black alligator boots. How he managed to look gallant and disreputable all at once she did not know. She only knew that standing so close to him was making her tingle in a way that was not in the least bit appropriate. "Then why are you still here?"

He stood, legs braced apart, arms folded in front of him. "Because, like most Texas gentlemen, I was brought up to never, ever, leave a lady in distress."

Ignoring the tension headache that had been dogging her all day, Maggie balled her fists at her sides and blurted out angrily, "Look, I can see you mean well, but I really can handle this."

His gaze moved over her in another long, thoughtful survey. "You sure seem to be doing a bang-up job so far."

No one had to tell her she'd made a terrible mess of things by once again allowing herself to be caught up and swept along by events that were oh-so-exciting at the time and oh-so-wrong for her later. But she was not about to tell any of that to the arrogant, infuriating man standing in front of her. Maggie admitted instead, "I just didn't want to get married, okay?" He shrugged and lifted his brow, seeming to reserve judgment on the workings of her fickle heart. "Nothing wrong with changing your mind," he said, quietly. Then, as if unable to resist, he added, "Even if your timing did suck."

Aware that she really was drawn to him, a fact that was as shocking as it was unacceptable, Maggie took another step back. She was not going to fantasize about what it would be like to feel the force of that much masculine confidence and testosterone. She was not going to wonder what it would be like to experience the skill of those big hands and sensual lips, or feel the weight of his body stretched over the top of hers. Not when what she really needed here was to be free.

Jerking in a stabilizing breath, she forced herself to return to the matter at hand. "Look, I know you're a man on a mission, but I just want to limit my embarrassment and get out of here."

He extended a hand. "Then come back up the mountain with me."

Maggie thought about everyone she had let down, the beautiful ceremony she had willfully—and wrongfully—ruined. And all because she didn't know her own mind. "Thanks, but no. I'm getting out of these woods on my own," she declared.

Another cool lift of the brow, as he regarded her with those gorgeous dark brown eyes. And then once again, he moved swiftly and patiently toward her.

HART WOULD HAVE preferred not to have to do this, but given the alternatives, he had no choice. Ignoring the runaway bride's swift gasp of dismay, he caught her against him, slid a hand under her knees, another behind her back and swung her up into his arms. The five-foot-seven brunette was every bit as supple, slender and feminine as she looked.

He'd carried heavier loads when he was in the army, but trekking back up the mountain with a woman struggling in his arms would be no easy trek.

The beautiful Maggie McCabe knew it, too, and used the notion to her advantage. She slammed a fist on his shoulder. "Put me down, before we both fall down, you big lug!"

He held her even tighter, assessing her all the while. There was no way he was dropping her, but there were also significant disadvantages to holding her soft, warm body so close—the least of which was what it was doing to his lower half. "Believe me, I wish I could. But since I have no desire to get lost in the woods and spend the night on the mountain with you, fending off armadillos and snakes…"

And way too much desire.

Her chin lifted defiantly. "One, you wouldn't

get lost because I'm betting you know this entire mountain like the back of your hand. And two, I'm not scared of Texas wildlife—I grew up with it." She wiggled restlessly in his arms, prompting an even fiercer rush of blood to his lower body. "So forget trying to scare me into behaving the way you want me to behave… 'cause I am *not* going with you!"

Not without a fight, anyway, he amended silently. Seething with an aggravation paramount to hers, he set her down. Trapping her slender frame between his big body and the broad, rough trunk of a century-old tree. "Okay, then we'll wait."

She studied him with glittering sea blue eyes. "For what?"

"You. To calm down."

Her glare deepened.

"And convince me that indulging in your diva drama is the right thing." When he was pretty damned sure, even without knowing all the details, that it wasn't.

She ripped off her tiara and veil. A scattering of pins followed, unleashing a riot of chocolate-brown curls that looked every bit as silky and delectable as the rest of her. "It is not diva drama!"

Aware this would have been amusing under any other circumstances, he took in the erotic disarray of her shoulder-length mane and tried not to think about what it would be like to kiss her. "Then what was it?" he asked, resisting the urge to reach out and restore some order to the unleashed strands.

Her lower lip trembled, and she offered a tight, officious smile. "You wouldn't understand," she said, finally.

And suddenly, he wanted to do just that. Which was odd, given he usually had little to no interest in other people's private business. Warning himself to get it together, Hart turned his attention away from her lusciously soft lips to the gradually slowing pulse in her throat. "I might. We'll never know unless you try me."

Another silence fell, this one more fraught with tension than the last.

Maggie pressed her lips together, took another deep breath and folded her arms across her chest. "I just *can't* get married," she confessed with another slow shake of her pretty head. She looked at him again, almost beseechingly this time. "I thought I could…but I can't."

Hart had seen that kind of unease before…in his own ex-fiancée. As he recalled, Alicia had been just as confused then as Maggie was now. "Why can't you?" he prodded, pushing away his own unhappy memories of a breakup he hadn't seen coming.

"Because I don't have it in me to promise to do one thing—like marry Gus—for the rest of my life."

On the surface, her excuse sounded shallow. Going a little deeper…

Hart thought about the relief he'd eventually felt when his own nuptials had been cancelled. The knowledge that what he had initially interpreted as disaster was really a very good thing in the end. "So what if you don't?" he countered, not about to judge her for that.

She peered at him curiously. "You're telling me that you don't believe in marriage, either...?"

Like her, he'd initially *thought* he did. Only to be saved by his bride-to-be, who'd had the good sense to call off a relationship that never would have lasted over the long haul, given their very different natures.

"No," he admitted abruptly, aware his ex had been right about one thing. He was too restless to ever settle down in one place for very long. "I don't."

Maggie blinked. She leaned closer in a drift of intoxicating perfume. "But your family owns a wedding business! How can you not believe in happily-ever-afters?"

Good question, Hart thought. And one his parents repeatedly asked him. Aware this wasn't the time to be discussing his issues, however, he moved the conversation back to her dilemma.

"Look, I don't know what happened to cause all this craziness. But I do know you can't keep running. Your family will forgive you…" They were, after all, part of the Texas McCabe clan, a family known for their devotion to one another.

Maggie scoffed "I don't think so. Don't forget. I didn't just ruin my wedding, I ruined my twin sister's nuptials, too."

"Not necessarily." At her astonished look, he continued, "I think Callie and Seth went on with it." At least he hoped they had. "And you have to go back."

"I agree," a low male voice said.

Maggie and Hart turned.

Gus Radcliffe stood at the top of the ravine. He looked the way Hart had felt the moment he got the "I Can't Do This After All" speech from his fiancée. Like he'd had the stuffing kicked out of him.

The dark-haired groom made his way down to where they were standing. "Come on, Maggie. I know you're mad at me for what I said after the rehearsal dinner, but you can't end a seven-year relationship over one difference of opinion."

They'd been together that long? Hart thought in shock. He tried to imagine it. Couldn't.

Maggie scowled. "I'm not."

Gus harrumphed in frustration. "Running out in the middle of the ceremony says you are. So, Magnolia, if your aim was to put me on notice for not being *enthusiastic* enough about your plans for our future, consider it done."

Ouch, Hart thought.

Maggie recoiled in shock, but fought back, just as fast. "Contrary to the way you seem to be remembering things, Gus, I never forced you into this. Or anything else, for that matter."

Her beau regarded Maggie skeptically. "Actually, you and your twin kind of did. Not that I'm protesting." Gus lifted a hand. "It never hurts to be practical, financially. And the truth is, you and I were destined to get married anyway. Might as well save your parents the cost of yet another wedding—when they still have four more ahead of them. While," he added importantly, "simultaneously letting you and Callie continue your tradition of doing everything together, as twins. Before that, too, comes to an end."

Hart watched as Maggie hauled in a deep breath. "Except I no longer want to do this," she pointed out.

Gus snorted and stood his ground. "I think you do. I think you're scared about the enormity of the commitment, same as me." His voice dropped consolingly. "But the thing is, Maggie, even if we disagree about a few of the fundamentals—"

"A few very important fundamentals."

"—we have to get married if we're going to start having kids together, the way we planned."

Maggie's slender shoulders lifted in another

careless shrug. "You and I don't have to be married for either of us to have kids, Gus."

"Meaning what?" Gus asked, clearly hurt. "You still want them, just not with me?"

A telltale silence fell. Maggie shivered, despite the heat of the late June day. "All I'm asserting is that it would be a huge error to bring children into an uncertain situation or an ill-fated marriage. Everyone knows that."

"That's the thing, Maggie," Gus returned quietly. "I don't think—despite our disagreement last night—that the two of us *are* making a mistake, getting hitched. And I certainly don't think we should let all the hard work and money we put into our nuptials be for naught. I think we owe everyone, especially our families, more than that."

There was another beat of silence. Finally, she lifted her hands guiltily. "You're right. I shouldn't be letting everyone down. And I should have realized how you felt long before now." She paused to work off her diamond engagement ring and forced it into Gus's hand. "Because if I had, I never would have said yes to your proposal. And if you had known how I felt about what our future should look like, you never would have asked me to marry you, either."

Gus palmed the ring she had given him. Finally, he seemed to recognize the truth of that. He sighed, slid the diamond in the inside pocket of his tuxedo jacket, then paused to look Maggie in the eye. "So you really don't want to go through with it?"

"I just can't," Maggie said softly. "Surely you understand that."

Even though Hart disagreed with the reckless, hurtful way Maggie McCabe was breaking her engagement, he had to admire her resolve. He had always liked a woman who was strong enough to stand up for what she wanted.

Squaring his shoulders, Gus looked at Maggie in grim resignation. "Then I'll go tell everyone." He headed off in the direction of the music from the string quartet.

Maggie turned back to Hart. Her elegant features were taut with a mixture of relief, guilt and grief. But mostly relief, Hart noted.

"Now, will you please take me back to the Double Knot ranch house?" Maggie asked.

It was Hart's turn to hesitate. "You're sure you don't want to go with Gus and make the announcement with him?" he prompted. "If we hurry, we could still catch up."

Maggie shook her head, abruptly an ice princess through and through. To the point Hart wondered what it would take to break down the impervious shield around her heart and find the real, unguarded woman underneath.

"Gus can handle it," she claimed with an indignant huff, thrusting out her kissably-soft, pink lower lip.

"True. But should he have to?" Maggie gave him another long, debilitating look that only made him want to kiss her even more.

With effort, Hart ignored the man-woman tension suddenly shimmering between them. Since when had he started thinking about what it would be like to chase some other guy's runaway bride? But here he was, wondering what it would be like to haul her close enough to feel her soft, sexy body pressed up against his and make that pout of hers disappear…

Maggie appeared to tense. "Look, Hart, I don't expect you to understand where I'm coming from here…but the fact is, I don't want to deal with our families when they're this upset with me." She folded her arms, gave him another pointed glance. "I'd rather face them after we've all had time to cool off—that way there's less of a chance of anyone saying something they can't take back."

That much, Hart did understand.

He had some air-clearing of his own to do with his parents, at evening's end. Worse, the news he'd come there to tell them would not be received happily. Which meant, like Maggie, he would likely be parting company with his folks tomorrow morning on less than ideal terms.

In the clearing above them, the music stopped abruptly, mid-tune.

Aware that his job—when he was at the ranch, helping out his parents—was to assist in seeing that every celebration held there went as flawlessly as possible, Hart tried to comfort Maggie. "I get wanting to run from unpleasant confrontations." He took another step closer. "But you're going to have to face the consequences sometime." He gave her a chance to ponder that notion. "Sooner rather than later might be easier." Ignoring his outstretched hand and offer of escort back to the party, Maggie flattened her palm across the center of his chest, and gave him a decisive push back, not stopping until he was well out of the bubble of her personal space.

"And I will offer my heartfelt apologies eventually," she vowed. "But I am *not* going to do it until I figure out how I'm going to honor my own obligations and reimburse everyone for their time, trouble and expense."

Accepting financial responsibility was a good first step to moving on from a pretty big mistake.

The sight of her in full, glorious temper—about to be a single lady again—was even better.

Appearing oblivious to the undeniable desire welling deep within Hart, she lifted a finger. Her gesture drew his attention to the lush fullness of her breasts, pressing against the tight, beaded bodice of her wedding dress.

"Because Gus was correct about one thing. We can't let our families pay for a wedding that never actually happened. And since I'm the one who called it off at the very last moment, I'm the one who's got to figure out a way to make things right. Not just for me," she murmured softly, looking long and deep into Hart's eyes, "but for everyone."

Chapter Two

Two years later...

"The prodigal son of Sanders Mountain is coming home. Today?" Callie Grimes asked.

Maggie settled into her desk chair at the Double Knot ranch house and pressed the phone to her ear. She and her twin sister might live two hundred miles apart, but they were still as close as ever. Whether she needed a sympathetic ear or someone to roll ideas off of, Callie was who she called. And when the widowed Callie needed a shoulder to lean on, Maggie was there for her, too. "That's what the message on the office voice mail said."

Just to be sure, she'd played it back several times, listening to the deep, husky timbre of Hart Sanders's voice while tremors of awareness went up and down her spine.

Deliberately, Maggie pushed away the memory of the last time she and Hart had seen each other. Although that momentous encounter would forever be emblazoned in her mind, she was no longer just considered a runaway bride around here. In fact, she was a valued employee-slash-Jill-of-all-trades who had also managed to work off her portion of the botched wedding. It had been important to her that her parents not be left saddled with that. Almost as important as finding a place where she could heal, away from the inquiring eyes and minds of her family. And the fact that she had helped out Fiona and Frank Sanders, in turn, after Hart had departed for a job in Los Angeles, was of comfort to her, too.

Clueless to Maggie's musing, Callie continued her inquisition. "And you're there alone?"

"Temporarily." She bit her lip. "I mean, I have prospective clients coming in later." But not until after Hart had indicated he would be arriving.

Callie's momentary silence indicated she was not fooled. "You're not going to bare your soul to him again…are you?" her sister persisted above the happy babbling of her one-year-old son, Brian.

Maggie barely stifled a groan. "Callie!"

"The last time you were alone with Hart Sanders was on your wedding day. And you poured your heart out to him then."

Don't remind me. I can't stop thinking about that day as it is. How kind he was. How sexy, how male. How personable, despite all the drama...

Never had she felt such pure animal attraction to another human being.

"I told you that was a mistake." Maggie pressed a palm to her flushed skin. "I was overwrought."

Callie laughed. "Don't you mean turned-on?"

Maggie drew a deep breath. Leave it to her twin to intuit her deepest, darkest fantasies. She massaged the tension from her temples. "I am *not* having this conversation with you."

"Mmm-hmm. Methinks my sister doth protest too much."

"Oh, please," Maggie huffed. "Stop conjuring up romance for me and go back to your adorable baby boy—"

Maggie heard the back door to the office complex open and shut. She covered the mouthpiece with her hand and spoke quietly into the phone. "And here he is."

"You call me later! I want a full report!"

Her pulse racing, Maggie quickly put the phone down. She sat forward in her chair and went back to tackling yet another prenuptial task for a client. And not a second too soon, either, as firm male footsteps and the sound of something being rolled—maybe a cart?— followed. Seconds later, a familiar face appeared in the portal.

Maggie blinked at the sight of the ruggedly handsome ex-soldier. Although she and Hart had talked—or was it flirted?—from time to time on the phone when he "accidentally" called her extension, she'd never imagined what it might be like for them to actually come face-to-face again.

"Hey." Ignoring the jolt of excitement coursing through her, Maggie rushed to fill the awkward silence. "What are you doing here?" she asked cheerfully.

Message or not, it wasn't like Hart to just drop in. Particularly since he and his parents had barely been on speaking terms the last couple of years.

In fact, things had been so tense between Hart and his folks since he had taken a job in Los Angeles that the two times Hart had returned to the ranch, Maggie'd taken advantage of the prior notice and arranged to visit her own family until Hart was gone.

No such luck now, though, Maggie thought, still feeling a little embarrassed to square off with the man who had chased her down on what admittedly had been the worst day of her life. Not that Hart seemed to be thinking about that, Maggie noted cautiously. Or anything else remotely connected to her, thank heaven.

Apparently oblivious to the conflicted feelings welling up within her, Hart faced her across the cluttered surface of her desk. Clad in an expensive olive green button-up, nice-fitting khaki pants and boots, he looked handsome and sexy. His sandy brown hair was still cut short enough to require little in the way of maintenance, although it was more stylish now. The taut, masculine angles of his face had been left unshaven. He also appeared unusually contained and exceptionally tired around the eyes, like he'd been travelling for what seemed forever to get there. Which, given the fact he accompanied his famous boss, Hollywood movie actress Monica Day, wherever her work took her, could certainly be the case.

"I came to see my folks," he said. Every taut inch of his tall, imposing frame was poised and ready in a way she'd never seen before. "Are they around?"

Maggie studied the sticky-sweet smear of what looked like apple juice on the shoulder of his expensive shirt, and lower still, what looked like ground-in-cracker debris. Maybe it had been a long flight. Maybe he'd sat next to…well, what did it matter.

Aware he was still in need of an answer, she said, "Ah—actually, no. Your mom and dad are on a cruise to New Zealand and Australia."

Briefly, Hart appeared stunned. "When will they be back?"

Maggie shifted her gaze upward, over the strong suntanned neck, to his intense sable brown eyes. He had the same devastating impact on her that he'd had the first time they'd met. "Ten days."

His brow furrowed in a way that said he was anything but pleased about that.

Maggie fought back her attraction and pushed on, "I gather you've got some time off, too?"

"A little over two weeks, yeah." He shrugged his broad shoulders restively. "I had something important—" He sighed. "I wanted to surprise them."

Maggie leaned back in her chair. "Well, you did that, all right."

He shoved a palm through his hair, looked around at the empty suite of rooms where The Wedding Train business was conducted. "I just assumed it being the height of the season, they'd be here."

Normally, they would have been, Maggie knew. Unfortunately, bookings were down almost twenty-five percent in the past two years. Sadly, for a lot of reasons, it wasn't looking to get any better. Not that she planned to get into any of that with Hart, who made it a habit to stay as far away from the family business as possible. She watched him tilt his head, as if listening in the direction of the hallway beyond. For the first time she wondered if it was possible he wasn't alone. Could he have brought a *woman* home to meet his folks? Was that part of the surprise? And if so, why did she suddenly have a pit in the bottom of her stomach?

"When is the next event?" Hart asked softly.

A brief rustling sound echoed in the silence of the hall.

Maggie watched as Hart tensed even more and doubled back, toward the door. Brawny arms still folded in front of him, he stuck his head around the opening and peered out.

"At the end of next week," she said.

She watched him frown, tense all the more, while still lingering there in the doorway looking at whatever was out there before finally turning back to her.

Drawing a deep, stabilizing breath, Maggie

gestured at the stack of ivory placards and calligraphy pens on her desk. "I'm prepping for the next wedding now."

He nodded. His expression indicated he wasn't really interested in the details, but still he asked, "What about the rest of the staff? Where are they?"

Another thorny question. There had previously been four full-time time employees in addition to herself and his parents, as well as a number of part-timers. "They still show up for events, but right now they are working other jobs," Maggie said.

"But you're here."

As the lone person on staff who had so little personal life she could afford to be constantly on call, Maggie confirmed lightly, "Twenty-four, seven."

This caught his attention "You're kidding, right? You're not really still living here on the ranch?"

Aware her accepting one of the guest suites

at the sprawling ranch house had initially been only a temporary measure, Maggie said stiffly, "Hate to break it to you, but yeah, I am."

He looked her over critically, head to toe. "You do realize you can't hide out here forever. Sooner or later you're going to have to face the fallout of your 'big mistake' and rejoin the world."

Leave it to Hart to be hopelessly blunt. "Thank you, Dr. Ruth," Maggie bit out sarcastically.

Mischief sparkled in his dark brown eyes. "Funny, I would have thought you would've referenced Dr. Phil. But Dr. Ruth works." He squinted. "You know you're blushing."

Probably because I just referenced a renowned sex therapist instead of a relationship expert. Maggie winced. "You have that effect on me."

He gave her another long, steady look. "Get you all hot and bothered?"

Ignoring the tautening of her nipples, she allowed sweetly, "Hot under the collar, maybe."

He chuckled, his eyes holding hers for a disreputably long moment. "I'm all for that, too."

Maggie held her breath to avoid releasing a wistful sigh. Reaction shimmered through her, along with a deep-seated need that had gone too many years without sating. The merriment in his eyes faded, replaced by something stronger, hotter, more provoking still.

Then, without warning, there was another faint noise in the hall.

Hart appeared to tense, and glanced in that direction again.

Hopelessly curious, Maggie rose and moved around the desk. If Hart Sanders did have a ladylove out there, and he'd been in here flirting with her, she really would kick him in the shin.

"What about you?" she asked casually, edging closer to the door. "Doesn't Monica Day have her new movie debuting all over Europe soon? Won't you be going with her to handle security?"

Hart shifted, his warrior frame deliberately blocking her exit to the hall. "Which is something else I need to talk to my parents about," he drawled.

Then there were *two* things that had brought him back to Texas—giving Maggie more food for thought. Although why any of this should matter to her, she didn't know. They might have shared a special connection the day she decided not to marry Gus, but in reality, they barely knew each other.

"What's the first item on your agenda?" she asked, as the faint rustling noises in the hallway steadily increased.

"This," Hart said shortly.

He walked out of the office, just as a long, loud, enraged wail broke the office silence. He returned with an adorable baby boy cradled in his arms.

MAGGIE COULD NOT stop staring. For one thing, the little fella, who looked to be approximately eighteen months old, appeared to have been crying for a good long time before drifting off to sleep. His forehead bore a crease on one side, where he had pressed against something. His big blue eyes were swollen and puffy, his cherubic little face an indignant red and streaked with a mixture of the same crumbly matter Hart had stuck to his shirt. The tyke's sandy brown curls were sticky and tangled, matted with what appeared to be a combination of spit-up, crushed crackers and apple juice. All in all, Maggie couldn't help but note, the baby boy in Hart's arms was having a terrible day. Evidenced by the way he continued to sob, as if his little heart were breaking.

Instinctively, Maggie drew nearer. She knew it was none of her business, and certainly not her responsibility, but she could not bear to see a little one in such distress. "Who is this?" she cooed, gently touching the back of the child's head.

"My son. Henry," Hart had to shout to be heard above the loud wailing.

Hart had a baby? Maggie thought in shock, resisting the strong maternal urge to take the tyke in her arms and soothe all his unhappiness away. *Since when?* "He apparently hates traveling," Hart continued, shifting the inconsolable little boy carefully in his arms. With his free hand, he dragged a stroller and diaper bag from the hallway. "And it feels like he's got a really soggy diaper."

No kidding, Maggie thought, looking at the dampness dripping out of the little boy's summer overalls onto Hart's shirt.

Deciding the time for politeness had passed, she said officiously, "Well, let's see what we can do about that." Maggie grabbed the diaper bag from the handle of the stroller and carried it over to a small sofa in the corner of her office. Then she plucked a rolled plastic mat from the bottom of the bag and laid it across the upholstery. After adding a few other essentials, she gestured for Hart to put his son down.

Henry, who had been struggling incessantly in his daddy's arms, went willingly onto the temporary changing area.

Maggie stepped back to let Hart do the honors.

A mistake.

Henry used the time to flip over onto his stomach and crawl swiftly to the other side of the sofa.

Worried he was going to fall off the edge and tumble onto the hardwood floor, Maggie dove after him. She caught Henry just as he neared the slipping point, and with her hands tucked gently but firmly about his midriff, she brought him up into her arms.

The baby stopped crying long enough to stare at her warily, as if thinking: Friend or Foe?

Maggie wrinkled her nose and said softly, "Hey there, Henry, I'm Maggie."

Henry shoved the thumb on his left hand into his mouth. He sucked it noisily. Still cradling him tenderly in her arms, she sat down on the sofa. "How about you and I get that soggy, wet diaper off, and maybe some clean clothes on, too," Maggie proposed softly. "So you'll be all comfy again." Gently, she placed Henry down onto the padded vinyl diaper-changing pad.

Ignoring the man to her left, who had backed up to give her room to work, Maggie kept her eyes on the baby. She could feel the intensity of Hart's attention, though, hot as a firecracker on the Fourth of July.... "What do you say, Henry?" Maggie let go of the tyke with one hand long enough to reach for the snaps on the legs of his overalls designed to make diaper changing easier.

She was *not* going to allow herself to fall in love with this cute little whippersnapper, the way she did every baby that came her way.

And she was certainly not going to fall for his equally good-looking daddy. It didn't matter how many times she'd thought of the rugged ex-soldier-turned-personal-security-expert since they last met.

"Are you up for it, little guy?"

Henry removed the thumb from his mouth, decision made. "No!" he said loudly and distinctly. He flipped onto his tummy again.

Maggie gently brought Henry back around. "Sure about that?" she teased, already working off her wristwatch with her free hand. She dangled it in front of him and continued in a cheery singsong voice. "I've got something for you."

Unable to resist the temptation of sparkling silver and gold, Henry reached for the accordion-style band. Maggie let him have it, and only when he was holding the wristwatch with both hands, avidly examining the face of it closely, did she quickly undo the snaps and ease the diaper off.

A short minute and a half later, Henry was good to go.

The boy was a little antsy, probably from being cooped up for too long. Maggie set him down on the floor and guided him to the open toy and play area adjacent to her office. He toddled happily into the carpeted area with the miniature chairs and table, obviously grateful for the chance to explore.

Satisfied the child would be fine for the moment, Maggie turned back to his daddy. And that was when she saw what Hart had been up to, too. She stared at broad shoulders and a very fine chest. Equally nice abs. And an arrow of dusky brown-gold hair sliding down into the waistband of his pants. She couldn't help the gasp that escaped from her lips. "You took off your shirt!"

He shrugged. "It was soaking wet and smelled like pee. What would you have me do?"

Maggie gulped, as her nipples tautened once

again. Lower still, there was an even more treacherous reaction. "Put on another?"

He met her chastising glance with a boyish, devil-may-care smile. "I would if I had one handy, but I don't." He peered at her closely. Moved nearer, too. "Why?" His seductive grin broadened. "Does the sight of my bare chest bother you?"

Maggie threw up her hands in aggravation. "Would the sight of my bare chest bother you?" she shot right back.

"Actually, now that you mention it..." He tilted his handsome head to one side, considered her a long, sensual moment. "I might enjoy the view.

Maggie was sure he would. "Well! This is *hardly* the time or place for this," she fumed. "Especially when you have a baby to take care of."

At the mention of Henry, Hart sobered. "You're right. This should come later."

And that was when the outer door opened,

and Maggie's next appointment of the day walked in.

For a moment, the affianced couple just stared, as if wondering what in the world they'd interrupted.

Then Hart flashed a sexy grin, and quickly discarded the soiled diaper. "My son had a little accident that somehow ended up on me, and Maggie was kind enough to help us out." Hart rolled the damp clothing up into a ball, tucked it under one arm, walked over to the play area and reached for Henry. "And now that she has," he said, "we'll get out of your way. And let the three of you get down to business."

LYNETTE JAWORSKI AND Ben Bauer were in their early twenties and, from the looks of it, head over heels in love with each other in a way that Maggie had never been.

Pushing aside her pang of envy, she offered them a seat, then said graciously, "I understand you're getting married next April and are considering the Double Knot as a venue."

Lynette took Ben's hand. "Actually, we're only here because my parents insisted we see it."

Outside, Henry began to wail. Maggie struggled to keep her mind on business.

Ben continued, "We don't want what happened to that one couple to happen to us."

There was no need to ask what Ben and Lynette were talking about; Maggie knew all too well.

Without warning, Hart walked back in, clean casual shirt on, a tearful Henry in his arms. The boy's lower lip quavered. He took one look at Maggie and held out his arms for her to come and get him.

Aware the choice was a full-blown toddler eruption or an interruption during the meeting, Maggie stood and walked over to Hart. The little boy vaulted into her arms, promptly stuck his thumb in his mouth and rested his head on her shoulder.

"Sorry about the interruption," Hart said, clearly not sorry at all, if it meant his little boy would get the maternal comfort he needed. "But Henry wanted Maggie."

"No problem." Lynette waved off the intrusion. "All little boys want their mommies."

Except I'm not his mommy, Maggie thought. *And I'm not going to be his nanny, either.* But not wanting to get into that, during what was turning out to be a not-so-easy sales pitch, she prompted instead, "So, you were saying...?"

"After reading everything in the reviews online, there's no way we would feel comfortable holding our wedding here, even if the Double Knot is where Lynette's parents were married," Ben said flatly. "So," they rose and headed hand-in-hand for the door, eager to be on their way, "thanks for meeting with us, Ms. McCabe, but no thanks."

They walked swiftly out the door. Seconds later, the exterior door banged shut.

Hart turned to Maggie, perplexed. "What was that about?"

"The malfunction of the steam engine, a year and a half ago. The train broke down as it was headed up the mountain. We had to transport the wedding party up to Nature's Cathedral by bus. The wedding ceremony itself went without a hitch, but the train still wasn't fixed, so everyone had to get back on the buses and drive down the old logging trails to the reception. Naturally, we apologized profusely for the inconvenience and the couple was given a hefty discount in compensation, but a number of the members of the wedding party were terribly upset, and they posted bad reviews about the Double Knot and The Wedding Train all over the place."

Hart slipped into business mode. "What's been the impact on the bottom line?"

"Not good." Contentment flowing through

her as Henry snuggled even closer against her, Maggie explained the subsequent lag in business.

"Can't anything be done to counter the negative reviews?"

Maggie decided not to sugarcoat the situation. "If your parents would agree to a social media presence, then, yes."

"You've tried to persuade them?" Hart guessed.

"A few times," Maggie admitted. "Callie is an expert in the field and could probably help us, but your parents don't want any part of it."

Hart shook his head in wordless disapproval. "Tell me about it! Since they aren't keeping up with the times, I tried to get them to sell the business and retire. But they refused. They wanted me to come in and take it over. They still do."

"But you're not interested," Maggie allowed, trying without success to figure out why the notion that Hart did not want to return to his home state of Texas was so upsetting to her. Given the sparks they drew off each other, she ought to want him as far away as possible.

"I'm grateful for the upbringing I had here and the people skills I learned from working in such a chaotic business, but it's not for me."

Honestly, Maggie couldn't see Hart managing the wedding business, either. A larger than life, big-picture guy like him would go crazy with the aesthetics and the minutiae. Sometimes, she felt like she might, too. "I understand. But that aside…" Aware she was loving holding the toddler a little too much, she handed Henry back to his dad. "You really can't barge in when I'm in the middle of a meeting."

Hart was instantly contrite. "I know—I'm sorry. I forgot to take the diaper bag with me and Henry's toys were in there. And once Henry heard your voice…"

Maggie took a seat behind her desk and retorted, "You couldn't have entertained him any other way?"

Smiling casually, Hart gave her a leisurely once-over. "Magnolia McCabe...are you accusing me of just wanting to commandeer your attention and spend time with you?"

Maggie flushed at his low, flirtatious tone.

With his smile widening and his son cradled tenderly against his chest, he inched closer. Maggie rocked back in her chair and tried to tamp down the immediate spark of excitement she felt. It took every ounce of self-control she had not to rise and join them both.

"Because it's really not true," Hart quipped. He sat on the edge of her desk, facing her. "It's Henry here, who is completely and utterly crushing on you." He indicated the winsome toddler. "Henry, whose heart you seemed to have captured."

It was easy to see the staggering resemblance between Hart and his son. Both were incredibly handsome and engaging, in their own way. Maggie felt something catch in her heart. She knew her need for connection went soul-deep.

But this was not the time or place to indulge that desire. Not when the child was so vulnerable.

She swallowed around the telltale tightness of her throat. "I know Henry likes me. I like him, too. But you can't keep treating me like his nanny."

Chapter Three

For a moment, Hart looked like he'd had his fair share of disappointments, too. He gave her a steely-eyed glare. "I'm not asking you to take responsibility for my son."

Maggie forced herself to keep her guard up, resisting the urge to become even more involved in what was, she knew, a very emotionally charged situation. And where was the child's mother, anyway? Who was she?

As if sensing the tension between the two adults, Henry squirmed unhappily in Hart's arms.

He awkwardly attempted to make his son

comfortable. Failed. "But with my parents not here, and me not knowing the first thing about taking care of a baby… Look, I just need you to show me what to do," Hart said, serious now. "Help me fix him something for dinner, get him ready for bed."

And then what? Maggie wondered. The three of them would be under the same roof, since her quarters were in the main house, too.

Not to mention the fact that with his parents away and the rest of the staff on hiatus at the moment, they were completely alone. And though Henry might work as an effective chaperone some of the time, he wasn't always going to be awake.

She ignored the fluttering in her middle. "You don't ask a lot."

"It's not for me." Hart set Henry down on the floor. Happily distracted, the toddler immediately walked off, exploring. "It's for him."

Maggie followed Henry into the hallway to

the door. She watched as the little guy stood on tiptoe, trying to work the doorknob.

This child was definitely going to be a handful.

Turning back to Hart, she folded her arms across her chest. "Shouldn't you already know how to do all this?"

He slung the diaper bag over his shoulder. "It's a long story."

"I've got time." Maggie opened the door for Henry. He toddled out, onto the long covered breezeway that connected the Double Knot Wedding Ranch offices to the sprawling cedar and stone ranch house. In the opposite direction, on the other side of the main house, the breezeway led to a four-car garage.

Ten acres away from that, on the other side of a beautifully landscaped flower garden and lawn, there was a train station built in the style of the Old West. There were covered platforms where guests sat as they waited to board the old-fashioned steam engine that would take them to Nature's Cathedral at the top of Sanders Mountain, a huge party barn where receptions were held and a large parking lot where wedding guests could park.

Maggie opened the back door to the house. "I mean, do your parents even know they are grandparents?" Maggie was pretty sure the intensely family-oriented Fiona and Frank would have mentioned it if they had.

Hart lifted up his son, and carried him across the threshold, before setting the little boy down again. "I just found out myself three days ago." Sorrow colored his low tone.

Shock rendered Maggie momentarily still. "Seriously?"

Hart set the diaper bag down on the hall table. "My ex-fiancée never told me she was pregnant." He shrugged, shook his head. "I might not have known at all if Alicia hadn't died in a car crash a month ago."

A silence fraught with heartache fell.

Maggie caught up with Henry, who was

headed for the back stairs. She grabbed the little boy's hand and turned him back in the direction of the ranch-house kitchen. "Where's Henry been since?" Together, the three of them entered the spacious room.

Maggie left Hart to keep track of his son, while she opened up the large, stainless steel fridge and got out the makings for the little boy's dinner.

"Foster care in Santa Fe, New Mexico. Apparently, my name was on Henry's Texas birth certificate, but between the bureaucracies of the two states, it took them a while to track me down."

Maggie set a skillet on the six-burner Viking stove and turned the heat to medium. "Poor kid." She buttered two pieces of bread and put a slice of American cheese between them.

Hart's forehead creased. "He was well cared for. At least he seemed somewhat happy, if pretty confused, when I went to pick him up. I thought it would be easier to fly to San Antonio, and then rent a car for the remainder of the trip." Hart scooped up his son before he could exit the kitchen at top speed. The two of them watched as Maggie spooned applesauce into a dish.

Maggie lifted the spoon to Henry's lips. "Since it's only a little over an hour from the city to the Double Knot." The child paused, thinking, then cautiously took a bite.

"Right. Unfortunately, while en route, we had to change planes in Dallas. Our flight was running late, and we barely made the connection. Henry didn't take well to the confusion and he absolutely hated takeoff and landing."

Maggie set the dish on the counter next to Hart and handed him the spoon so he could do the honors. "Probably his ears."

Hart shifted Henry to his left arm and picked up the spoon with his right hand. "What?"

A little too aware of how cozy and domestic this all felt, Maggie poured milk into a cup.

"The change in air pressure is hard on their little ears."

A corner of his mouth took on a downward slant. "Makes sense. Anyway, he was really miserable and really ticked off. He wouldn't stay in his safety seat next to me, and he was worse on my lap. He cried the entire time."

Maggie's heart went out to both of them. They couldn't have had a worse start to their trip or their relationship.

"And he was even madder when we picked up the rental," Hart mused as he continued feeding his son the last of the applesauce. "Fortunately, he fell asleep about forty minutes into the drive and was still snoozing when we got here."

Noting the sandwich was done, Maggie slid it onto a plate and began slicing it into small kid-sized squares. "So you put him in his stroller."

Hart nodded while they waited for the grilled cheese bites to cool. "And wheeled him into the house, thinking my mom and dad would be here."

Only to find me instead, Maggie thought.

She dampened a paper towel and used the edge of it to clean the applesauce from around Henry's mouth. "This is why you were hoping to surprise your parents." The little boy lurched toward Maggie. She caught him in her arms.

"I figured it would be better to tell them in person."

A tenuous silence fell. "Are you still going to wait for that? Or let them know now?"

Hart hesitated. "I hate to disrupt their trip, knowing how long they have wanted to see that part of the world and how seldom they treat themselves to a vacation, but I really need them to help me get Henry settled. So, looks like I'll be emailing them the news tonight."

Maggie pulled a chair up to the table, put the sandwich in front of her and sat down with Henry on her lap. She offered him a bite. "How do you think they'll react?"

For a second, Maggie didn't think Hart was going to answer. Sorrow came and went in his eyes. Finally, he pulled up a chair next to them and allowed, "I'm sure they'll be surprised and happy to find out they have a grandson. However, they won't be as happy about my part in the snafu."

If there was one thing Maggie understood all too well, it was not meeting parental expectations. Compassion welled within her. "You think they'll blame you, for not knowing?"

"Hard to say," Hart said quietly, offering his son another bite of grilled cheese. "What I do know is that my mom and dad had reservations about my engagement to Alicia from the get-go."

His romantic past was more complicated than she realized. That gave them something in common in that respect, too. "Frank and Fiona didn't like Alicia?"

Hart caught Maggie's confused look. "They thought I might not be right for her."

"Why not?" she asked, shifting Henry onto Hart's lap and going to get the little boy a drink.

"Alicia was a small-town Texas girl and she wanted stability."

Maggie washed out the baby bottle from the diaper bag and filled it with milk. She paused to give it to Hart, then stood opposite him, her back to the marble counter. "And you couldn't give that to her."

Hart's lips compressed grimly. "I tried. It's why we got formally engaged when I still had a year and a half left to go on my tour. Because she needed to know I was serious, that I intended to marry her when my military commitment was up."

"What happened?"

"She was frustrated because I didn't know what I wanted to do when I got out of the service—except not come back here to live. And I didn't want to set our wedding date until I knew what I was going to be doing, where we were going to live." Frustration glimmered in his dark brown eyes. "So she called it off. Said I was too restless to ever settle down in one place, and that was all she'd ever wanted."

Finding his steady regard a little unnerving, Maggie set the skillet in the sink, squirted dish-washing liquid into the center of it and got to work. "Did you have any qualms about leaving the military?"

Hart shook his head. "No. When I'm ready to move on, I move on. I don't spend a lot of time looking back. And although I enjoyed my time in the armed forces and felt good about serving my country, I was ready to try something else."

Maggie understood that, too. It was why she had gone from business analyst to wedding planner. Because—even though this wasn't something she planned to do permanently—she had needed a change.

Another silence fell. Henry having finished his dinner, Hart brought him over to the sink and Maggie helped him wash the child's face and hands. Then Hart set him down on the floor, in front of the bay window in the breakfast nook. Henry stood, his hands pressed against the glass, looking outside.

Hart stood next to his son, tenderly standing guard. Watching them together, Maggie could already feel the love flowing from father to son.

She shook her head. "I don't understand why Alicia wouldn't have told you about the baby."

"I don't understand it, either. Unless it was because she wanted to keep Henry all to herself." He paused. "She had to have known that I wouldn't have just walked away. I would have insisted on shared custody."

Maggie moved closer. "I'm sorry she didn't tell you. It was wrong of her to keep him from you."

Hart reached out and squeezed Maggie's hand. "Thanks for saying that."

It wasn't just a platitude. It bothered her that

he thought it might be. "I mean it, Hart. You were dealt a raw hand. You didn't deserve it."

Another moment passed. They exchanged fragile smiles while Maggie considered the irony that Hart had helped her out in the midst of the worst crisis of her life, to date. Now, she was helping him out, in the midst of his.

"In the meantime," Hart drew a deep breath, considering. "I've got to figure out where Henry's going to sleep tonight."

He was watching her curiously, as if trying to read her mind while she worked to keep her emotions out of it. "Do you have a crib?"

Hart scrubbed a palm across the day's growth of beard on his chin. "Not sure." He frowned again. "There used to be one—mine, actually—in the attic. Would you mind looking after Henry while I go check it out?"

"Not at all." In her view, the sooner they got the little one down for the night, the better. And to that end…maybe she should speed things along, too.

"So what do you think, little fella?" Maggie asked, lifting Henry into her arms after Hart disappeared. The boy smiled and cuddled against her while Maggie ran her fingers through his cracker-and-juice-encrusted hair. Knowing his dad's chore was going to take a while, given the jumbled state of the contents of the attic, she asked, "You up for a bath tonight? Because to be honest, sport, you really need one."

Henry flashed a toothy grin.

"I'll take that for a yes," Maggie said. She retrieved the diaper bag, Henry still snuggled safely in her arms, and went up the stairs.

HART HEARD THE wild giggles the moment he hit the second floor. He followed the sound to the guest-room bath. Henry was in the tub, splashing happily. Maggie was kneeling in front of it, one hand tucked securely around Henry's tummy while Henry dropped a set of toy keys into the bubbles. Chortling happily, he picked them up and promptly dropped them again.

She certainly had the touch with kids, Hart thought. And she was still damned beautiful, too—even in disarray. In deference to the potentially messy task of bathing his son, she'd swept her thick espresso curls up into a loose knot on the back of her head. Her legs and feet were bare, her skirt pulled tight across her delectable derriere and hiked partway up her even more sensational thighs. The front of her blouse was damp and covered with bubbles. She looked as happy and relaxed as the toddler in front of her.

Was this the same child he had picked up at foster care that morning? Hart could hardly believe it.

Catching sight of him in the mirror, Maggie shifted slightly to look at him. As she moved, the neckline of her blouse gaped, showing a hint of lace and soft womanly curves. There was a light in her eyes that made his pulse race all the more.

"How did it go?" Her silky voice caressed his skin.

He kept his eyes on hers and Hart answered her smile with one of his own. "I found the crib. Unfortunately, it was covered with layers of dust."

"Did you bring it down?"

Hart edged nearer and caught a whiff of her perfume. Hyacinth. He repressed a sigh of pure lust. It had been a long time since he'd been with a woman. Too long. "I took it outside and hosed it off," he replied, trying in vain to get his libido under control and his mind back on track. "I was hoping that a simple rinse would do it, but it looks like it's going to need soap, too."

"I think there's some wood-oil soap under the kitchen sink."

Was it his imagination, or was it getting hot in here? "Thanks. I'll look." She seemed very much in her element with his child, amazingly so. "Are you okay here with Henry—if I go off to finish the job?"

Maggie nodded. "None of us will get any shut-eye tonight unless Henry has a place to sleep. So go for it."

"Thanks. I owe you."

She laughed and waggled her brows facetiously. "I'll remember that."

Hart took another last, lingering look at the two of them, then went off to finish the chore. By the time he returned, Maggie was in the living-room rocking chair, Henry on her lap. The baby had a bottle of milk clutched in his hands, and he was drinking it drowsily. The two looked like mother and son, and Hart couldn't help but smile at them. Maggie smiled back, then stiffened abruptly. Her contentment fading, she seemed more than ready to relinquish his son to him. "All set?" she asked.

Hiding his regret to see her so eager to leave, Hart nodded. "Bed's made and everything."

Maggie rose, Henry still in her arms. "Where'd you put it?"

"My old room."

"Ah, yes." Her blue eyes sparkled with mischief. "The one with all the trophies and awards."

A little embarrassed his parents insisted on keeping the room like a museum of his accomplishments, Hart dipped his head in droll acknowledgment. "That would be the one."

"You know, it might be a good idea to take the rocking chair up there."

Hart had been thinking the same thing. Wordlessly, he handed Henry back to Maggie. Then picked up the rocker and headed up the stairs. Maggie and Henry followed along behind him.

When they reached his old bedroom, Maggie looked approvingly at the crib set up right next to the extra-long twin bed of his youth. A bedside lamp was glowing. Once again, she relinquished command of her young charge.

"Ten more minutes of rocking and he ought to be out like a light."

Hart nodded his understanding. Trying not to think how quickly he had come to rely on her, he sat down with Henry in his arms and got to it.

HALF AN HOUR LATER, Maggie was in the kitchen making tortilla soup and a salad for her own dinner when Hart walked in. He had changed into a pair of nice-fitting jeans and a denim shirt, and for the first time since he had arrived, he looked completely relaxed and at ease.

She couldn't help but light up at the sight of him.

He was just so damned sexy.

And she could not afford to be noticing!

Maggie tabled the loneliness that made her so susceptible and brought her thoughts back to the situation at hand. "Henry asleep?"

Hart breathed a sigh of relief. "Yeah." His

smile grew tender. "He fought it as hard as he could, but the poor little guy just couldn't keep his eyes open. I put him in his crib about ten minutes ago, and he ought to be good for a while. In the meantime, I rigged up a make-shift baby monitor by calling the house phone with my cell and leaving the phone receiver in Henry's room. I hope that's okay," he said.

Impressed he had figured out what to do until they could get a real baby monitor for him to use, Maggie nodded her approval. "If anyone really needs me, they'll call my cell phone." She paused. "I'm glad he's finally asleep, though."

Except…it would mean they'd have the rest of the night without distraction. And the two of them needed the commotion Henry supplied to keep them safely at arm's length.

Hart strode closer. He'd shaved since she had seen him last. A mixture of mint and spicy af-tershave lotion clung to his handsome jaw. She felt a tingle of awareness deep inside her.

He smiled. "But just in case—would you

mind keeping an ear out for him while I bring in the stuff from the rental car?"

"No problem." It would give her a moment to calm her jumping nerves.

"Thanks." Hart flashed a confident smile, promising, "It should just take a couple of minutes."

While he was gone, Maggie got out two bowls, a bag of chips and some grated cheddar. She didn't really want to eat dinner with Hart—it somehow felt a little too intimate—but she also knew he had to be hungry. Good manners dictated she share what she had, at least for that evening. The fact she'd felt something for him, when they were talking, had nothing to do with it. Nor did the fact she found him as tempting as ever.

Hart came back in, loaded down with a big suitcase prominently bearing Henry's name, an expensive leather duffel with his initials and a laptop bag.

He grinned when he saw the double place-setting at the kitchen island. "Expecting company or is that for me?"

"It's for *us*," she corrected wearily, then aware of the potential implications of that, quickly wished she hadn't. "And you are 'company' to me, in the strictest sense of the word."

She meant to reassure him. Put the mood back in the platonic-to-a-fault category. Instead, to her frustration, her words had the opposite effect. His dark brown eyes lit up the same way they had when she'd mentioned Dr. Ruth instead of Dr. Phil. He invaded her space, wrapping both hands around her spine. "Sure about that?"

He pressed lightly, bringing her all the way against him. Now she was the one on fire with desire. Her pulse pounding, Maggie worked to get air into her lungs. "Hart…"

"Can't help it, Maggie," he said huskily, guiding her closer still. "I've been wanting to kiss you since the first time I saw you. And damned if I'm not going to do just that."

Chapter Four

Hart had been telling himself that the memories of that day, long ago, were greatly exaggerated. That it had just been the excessively emotional nature of the encounter that had him thinking about her again and again and again.

That theory was soon proved completely wrong when instead of resisting, she went up on tiptoe, more than meeting him halfway. Her arms wreathed his neck, the soft warmth of her breasts pressed against his chest and she let out a whisper of a moan as their lips met. The sweet taste of her rocked him to his core. He cupped one hand beneath her jaw and slid his other through the thick silk of her hair until he had tilted her head just so. Until she was kissing him back with all the heat and passion he had expected her to have. Making him want. Need. Yearn to have her beneath him.

And it was then, when he was pulling her up against him, sliding his palms down her spine to the small of her back, letting her warmth wash over him, that she kissed him all the deeper.

Maggie knew she shouldn't have gone so willingly into his embrace, and she certainly shouldn't be kissing Hart like this. But there was something about him that had her drowning in his eyes and feeling so damned alive.

Perhaps it was the way he looked at her. As if there was nothing more important than the here and now. As if he wanted to know as much about her as she yearned to know about him, even as his lips moved against hers, testing, discovering, until she gasped in sheer pleasure. Until kissing was an act in itself that could lead to so much more.

And that, Maggie knew, neither of them was ready for.

Calling on every ounce of self-preservation she possessed, she broke off the kiss and pushed him away. "We can't do this."

He mocked her with a glance even as he refused to budge. "Kiss?"

So, for him, it wasn't that big a deal. Another big warning sign. "Start something when you're in as much a state of crisis as I was the last time we met."

He cocked his head, regarding her with disbelief.

Maggie pulled herself together and rushed on, "I mean, I can be there for you as a friend. But beyond that, you can see how foolish it is to have a relationship that is anything but platonic."

PLATONIC, HART REPEATED to himself. Oh, man, could his week get any better? He let his gaze drift over her soft, damp, kiss-swollen lips. The pretty color in her cheeks. And the evasion in her blue eyes. "I see how foolish *you* think it is."

Her gaze met his, clear now. "You've got too much on your plate right now," she insisted.

Hart knew what would make him feel better. And it wasn't keeping his distance from the most compelling woman he'd ever come across in his entire life. "Or not enough, as the saying goes," he murmured, tempting her with a wicked smile.

Because now he saw, whether she realized it or not, that she needed to move on with her life—or risk being stuck in this rut forever. He cared about her too much to see that option materialize.

As if reading his mind, she blew out an aggravated breath, letting him know with a glance she wasn't the kind of woman who could handle sex with no strings. "Hart—"

Raising his hands in surrender, he backed up, reluctantly all Texas gentleman again. If he wanted her—and he did—two things were going to have to happen. One, it was going to have to mean something. And two, he was going to have to be patient. "Okay. Point taken." He laid a hand across his heart. "I promise I won't kiss you any more today."

She planted her hands on her hips and sent him a withering glance. "Funny. But that isn't the kind of pledge I was looking for."

"Me either, truth to tell." He'd wanted much more from her. Still did. "In the meantime…" Maggie was right about one thing, there were things that needed his immediate attention. He opened up his case and set his laptop computer on the counter. "Mind if I send off a quick email to my folks, before we eat? I'd like to let them know what's going on."

"No problem." Looking happy to move on to

something less problematic than the attraction between them, Maggie filled two glasses with iced tea and added sprigs of fresh mint. "What are you going to say to them?"

Hart sighed. *As little as possible.* "Just that I have some great news to share. And to call me as soon as they can."

Maggie leaned against the counter, sipping her drink. She studied him from beneath a fringe of thick dark lashes. "I'm sure they're going to be ecstatic when they find out they have a grandson."

Hart imagined that was true. He also knew the conversation likely wouldn't end there. His parents would lament being shut out of the first year and a half of Henry's life. They'd also want to know what Hart's plans were. All he knew for sure, as he plugged his cell phone and charger into the wall, shut his laptop and took a seat at the island, was that his initial idea—of having his parents temporarily help care for his son—was a bust. Which meant he was going to have to come up with a new one, fast.

His mood suddenly pensive, he watched as Maggie carried their dinner to the table. Hart was hungry and the home-cooked meal hit the spot. "This is incredibly delicious."

She smiled shyly. "Thanks."

He finished what was in his bowl, then got up to get another serving, before sitting down next to her once again. "I mean it. I'm not much of a soup guy, but this—" he spooned up a bite of tender chicken, floating in a rich broth, redolent with tomatoes, peppers, onions and black beans and garnished with cheese and crispy tortilla strips. "This is a meal."

She chuckled. "It's my parents' recipe."

Eager to know more about her and what her life had been like as a kid, he lifted a brow. "They both cook?"

Maggie wrinkled her nose. "No choice when there are six kids in a family and both parents work."

Hart thought back to the wedding. "That's right. You have six sisters, don't you?"

"A set of twins, a set of triplets and a single birth."

"All of you named after flowers?"

Maggie groaned. "Don't remind me. Being called Magnolia was the bane of my youth."

Hart recalled the lacy garter of silk magnolia blossoms she'd worn on her wedding day. His wish to be the one to be able to inch it down her long, lusciously shaped leg. "I don't know. I think it kind of suits you."

"You sound like my parents."

"They're doctors, aren't they?"

Maggie smiled. "My dad is a general surgeon. My mom is a pediatrician."

"Is that why you're so good with kids?" Hart asked curiously.

She shook her head and scooped up the last bite of broth-soaked tortilla chip. She got up and went to the fridge, returning with a bowl of freshly cut-up peaches, a can of whipped cream and two dessert dishes. "I babysat all through junior high and high school, and then became a nanny during the summer while I was in college."

Nanny. Now there was a good idea. If he could convince her to build on the loving rapport she'd already developed with Henry. "Ever think of going back to it?" he asked casually, beginning to wish he hadn't kissed her earlier. Especially if it messed up his long game.

"No." Their gazes met and she inhaled deeply. She scooped peaches into the dishes, then poured generous amounts of whipped cream onto the fruit. "I like being a business analyst."

"That's not exactly what you're doing here, is it?"

Maggie stiffened abruptly, her hand briefly touching his as she handed over the last course. "You're right. I'm more of a Jill-of-all-trades, as well as assistant manager for the Double

Knot Wedding Ranch business. But this is only temporary."

So she kept saying every time he razzed her on it. Which was, as it happened, every time they spoke on the phone.

"Still not tired of remaining at the scene of the um…abandoned vows?" he asked, taking a bite of some of the delicious fruit.

She looked at him for a long, quelling moment. "Staying here was for the best, all around," she said.

Hart moved his gaze from her silky soft lips and focused on the tumult in her pretty blue eyes. "Maybe it was best in the beginning when you were working to pay off the debt and hiding out from your family and ditched groom, but your bill has been paid for a while now. Hasn't it?" Maggie focused on her dessert. Finally, she swallowed, dabbed the corners of her lips with her napkin. "I'm not ready to leave just yet. Maybe in the fall, if your parents can find a replacement for me, but nothing is definite."

Silently, she pushed back her chair. He stood to help her with the dishes.

They both reached to open the dishwasher at the same time. Their shoulders and arms brushed before they could draw back. She sucked in a little breath, her eyes widening in a way that let him know she was physically aware of him, too.

Wishing he could kiss her again—without driving her further away than she was at this moment—he stepped back, to give her the physical space she craved.

Knowing nothing would be solved by pretending there wasn't a problem, he asked, "Why isn't anything definite?"

She moved past him with a glare. "Because I don't know what I want to do next."

He watched her clear the table with the ease of someone who had helped out at many a reception and rehearsal dinner. She set the tall stack in the sink. As she turned to face him, her hip brushed his. Not so accidentally this time. More to push him out of the way.

He stayed his ground, and blocking her now, he began to fill the dishwasher, despite her obvious wish to do so herself. "What about where you were working and living before you married Gus?"

She put the whipped cream and leftover soup back in the fridge. "Dallas?"

"Yes. Why didn't you go back there when you decided not to marry Gus?"

"For starters, I had no place to live, since Gus and I had been sharing a house with Callie and Seth in the year leading up to the wedding. We had planned to get separate places, once our lease was up, but in the meantime I couldn't live with Callie and Seth and spoil their happiness. Gus felt the same way. He moved out immediately, too."

Hart took the soiled pot and filled it with soapy water, while she grabbed the spray cleaner and a cloth and began wiping down the counters. "But you had a job—"

"Which was even worse, because at that time, Gus and I worked at the same company. A number of our coworkers were at the ceremony. Going back to that would have meant facing all the gossip." Finished with her task, she turned to him and wearily recounted, "It just seemed simpler to start over somewhere else. So, when your parents found themselves shorthanded after you left for Los Angeles, I volunteered to fill in to work off my wedding debt."

"And decided to stay."

Abruptly, tears glistened in her eyes. "It was quiet here. Between weddings, anyway." She leaned against the counter and dropped her gaze to the floor. "I needed to think. And it was far enough away from my family, and Gus's, so I didn't have to deal with their anger. Up close, anyway."

Hart dried his hands on a towel and approached her. Standing opposite her, he said quietly. "That was two years ago. Surely you can stop punishing yourself and finally move on."

Her chin lifted. "I'm not punishing myself."

He gave her a look that had her gazing away again. "My point is, surely there are other options for you now," he said quietly.

MAGGIE STARED AT HART, not sure why her well-being was so important to him. Just instinctively knowing that it was, and maybe always had been.

Not sure she wanted to be that important to anyone, never mind shake up her life the way he and his infant son were threatening to do, Maggie took a deep breath and walked outside onto the stone patio. The summer air was warm and clear. In the distance, Sanders Mountain loomed. In the other direction was another mountain owned by a neighboring ranch. It was also covered with trees, most of them pine.

For now, all was silent.

Except for the occasional sound of the birds and the wind.

And the man coming up behind her.

He set his cell phone, serving as his baby monitor, on the table. Straightened. "You were talking about your options.

Feeling restless, Maggie moved a short distance away on the stone patio and sat down on one of the wooden chairs. "Well, if you must know, my parents want me to come back to my hometown of Laramie and find a job there. Possibly with the hospital. Or their thriving medical practices."

Hart drew up a chair and settled in front of her. His dark brown eyes took in everything. "But you're not sold on the idea."

The look on his face was so understanding, Maggie began to relax, despite herself. "Gus is living there now. In the end, he had to leave Dallas, too. It was just too uncomfortable."

"So, if Laramie is out, what are your other options?" he pressed.

She let out a slow breath. "I went to college in Austin, so I might go back there." Restless again, Maggie stood and began to pace. She stopped at the edge of the patio and stared down at the flowers. Reminded of her wedding, she swung away from the prodigious blooms. "Or maybe San Antonio. Wherever I can find a job. It all sort of depends on how my parents react to the rest of my plans."

He came closer, too. "Which are what? Come on." He put his hands lightly on her shoulders, then bent so he could see into her face. "I can tell you have something concrete in mind."

Maggie bit down on an oath. What was it about this man that had her constantly revealing herself in a way she hadn't in…well, she couldn't remember when.

Figuring it couldn't hurt to let Hart know the truth, she bit out, "I'm going to have a baby."

For a moment, he was every bit as speechless as she had figured he would be. Eventually, his concerned glance drifted to her taut tummy. "You're pregnant?" His voice was low, husky, almost reverent.

To the point, she almost wished she was.

"No," Maggie responded quickly, "but I want to be."

His brow furrowed. He dropped his hands and stepped back. "Don't you have to date someone for that to happen?"

Maggie flushed at his needling tone. "Ha, ha. And how do you know I'm not dating someone?"

"Well, for starters, the fact you're still living here with my folks. It seems as if you were seeing someone, even casually, you would want more privacy."

He was right about that. Quietly, she revealed, "I'm more interested in having a baby on my own at this point."

He moved closer as dusk fell all around

them. It was beginning to feel far too romantic out here.

"You still don't want to get married?" he asked.

"In a perfect world, with the perfect man?" *Someone like say...you? If you were the settling down kind?* Which, she knew very well, Hart was not.

He shook his head and let out a low laugh. "Why would he have to be perfect?" As if that were the most boring thing on earth.

"Perfect for me," Maggie explained.

"Ah."

She studied his chiseled features, thick sandy brown hair and dark eyes. Physically, anyway, Hart was masculine perfection come to life. "But...you think that's unrealistic thinking, too."

He inhaled deeply, considering. Ran a hand through his hair. Finally, he reached out and took her hand. "I'm sure the right guy is out there, somewhere."

"Spoken like the son of parents who put on more than a few weddings."

He squeezed her fingers, then let her go. "Actually, all those weddings are probably why I'm not romantic."

"Because you've seen too many bridezillas?"

Hart wandered to the edge of the patio and gazed up at the moon. Three-quarters full, it shone against the backdrop of the increasingly dark, star-filled sky. "And indifferent grooms." He wheeled back to face her with an easy smile.

"Ah," Maggie noted playfully, glad the focus of their conversation was now on him. And his flaws. "So you are a cynic, at heart."

He chuckled. "And you're not?"

"I guess I am."

But I wish I wasn't, Maggie thought, returning Hart's rueful smile as he collected his cell phone and the two of them went back inside.

To Hart's disappointment, Maggie disappeared soon after that. She said she was going back to the office to finish up the calligraphy place cards she had been working on when he arrived. He knew it was because she didn't want to risk being alone with him. Or risk another kiss.

Hart knew putting distance between them was the smart thing to do. So he went upstairs to check on Henry.

The little tyke was still in the position Hart had left him, still sleeping soundly. He lingered in the doorway, content for a moment to just stand there, drinking it all in. It had been a hell of a few days, starting with the phone call from social services. But tough as it had been, he couldn't say he regretted anything except the fact he was so inept as a dad. He was going to have to do better.

Going to have to stop leaning so heavily on Maggie.

Downstairs, there was an urgent email from his boss, asking him to call her the first chance he got. Not ready to talk about his immediate plans, mostly because he had no clue what they were, Hart did not reply.

His computer chimed softly again.

The email icon lit up. This time with a message from his parents.

MAGGIE WAS NEARING the end of the stack of place cards, when the door opened.

Hart strode in, phone to his ear. "Yes, she's right here." Hart handed Maggie his cell. "My folks want to talk to you about business." He was out the door again and on his way back across the breezeway to the main house before she finished saying hello.

Frank got right down to brass tacks. "Hart told us the Jaworski's daughter and her fiancé stopped by today. He didn't seem to think the initial meeting had gone particularly well. Is that your assessment, too?"

The wedding was going to be a big one, and Maggie knew how much the Sanders had been hoping to continue the Jaworski family tradition and host it at the Double Knot. Still, she had to be honest. "The bride and groom are concerned about the train breaking down again. I did my best to reassure them it's only happened once, but it didn't seem to help."

Fiona tsked. "The senior Jaworskis have their hearts set on having their daughter married in Nature's Cathedral, just as they were."

Knowing what was expected of her, Maggie promised, "I'll see what I can do."

Frank and Fiona thanked Maggie for pitching in with Hart and the baby, and then rang off, promising to see them all soon.

Figuring she could finish the calligraphy in the morning, she turned off the light. Wondering how Hart's conversation with his parents had gone and what their reaction had been to the news about their new grandson, she picked up Hart's cell phone and headed back across the breezeway to the main house.

Hart was in the guest room adjacent from the one where Henry was sleeping. His briefcase was out, computer on. A folder of what looked like travel itinerary was spread out across his lap and the queen-sized bed. He appeared to be working. She handed him his phone, which suddenly started blaring Monica Day's new movie theme song.

Aware that wasn't the first time she'd heard that particular ring tone coming from his cell phone, Maggie asked curiously, "Aren't you going to answer that?"

"No." He shut it off completely, set it on the bedside table, then reached out and caught her wrist. "Can we talk?"

Maggie ignored the tingling in her arm. She slid out of his light grasp. "About?" She leaned against the bureau opposite him.

"The next couple of months. I know you said you were planning on leaving the ranch in the fall, but if we were to move that timetable—"

Uh oh. She had been afraid of this, since the first time Henry cuddled close. She put up a staying palm. "Please don't ask me that."

He cocked his head. "Ask you what?"

Maggie knotted her hands in front of her. "To be your son's nanny."

A long thoughtful pause followed. There was no telling what he was thinking. "Would you consider that?" he asked finally, a hopeful light coming into his sable brown eyes.

"No. I wouldn't." For so many reasons. The least of which was her hopeless ever-present attraction to him.

His broad shoulders relaxed slightly. In disappointment? Or relief? "That's what I thought."

"Then you *weren't* going to ask me that?"

Hart shook his head. "Nope." Putting aside some of the papers that she now saw were some sort of European tour itinerary, he leaned toward her and continued in a low tone. "On the contrary, I want you to stay on as assistant manager for however long you're needed, so my parents can return to California with Henry and me."

He sure wasn't procrastinating. But then,

he never had. When he wanted something, he went right after it. When he needed to leave, he left. And, as he'd indicated before, he did not waste any time looking back.

She swallowed, wishing Hart didn't constantly put her on edge. "Your parents agreed to that?"

His gaze narrowed. "They will if they think the ranch is in good hands during their absence. And it will be," he said, matter-of-factly, "if you're in charge."

In the pause that followed, she allowed herself to admire the width of his shoulders and the flex of his muscles beneath his soft chambray shirt. He might work in Hollywood these days, as his clothes earlier had attested, but he was still very much a Texas cowboy, too. Still very much a man who always found a way to simultaneously honor his commitments and succeed in whatever task he set for himself.

Right now, that agenda obviously did not include seducing her. But what if that changed? What if she wanted to seduce him?

Hart stared at her, perplexed. "What are you thinking?"

"Honestly?" Maggie jerked in a deep enervating breath. "That I don't want to make the same mistake that I made before."

Chapter Five

Hart knew he was rushing Maggie. Given the pressure on him, he didn't have much choice. "And what mistake was that?"

Regret pinched the corners of her mouth. "The one I always seem to make. I get completely swept up in whatever is going on around me and jump on the bandwagon, too. Usually to regret it later."

Hart cleared the papers off the bed and motioned for her to sit down opposite him. "And in this case?"

Reluctantly, she perched on the edge, a good distance away from him. "You and Henry and your folks are the bandwagon."

Maggie rubbed idly at the cotton fabric of her skirt, where it stretched across her thigh. With a sigh, she lifted her gaze to his. "Gus and I lived together on our own for a couple of years first. And of course my parents hated it. They said if we loved each other enough to live together, we should make it legal."

"So Gus proposed?"

"Not right away. But once Callie and Seth got engaged—there just wasn't any reason for us not to get engaged, too. And you pretty much know the rest." She sighed again, even more ruefully this time. "I got hopelessly caught up in the excitement of planning a wedding, only to realize at the very end that all I had done was jump on someone else's bandwagon. Again."

He shifted his glance away from her voluptuous breasts pressing against the front of her blouse. "I don't think this qualifies."

She rose abruptly. "My whole job, my presence here, my decision to stay on indefinitely, qualifies. As you pointed out earlier. And you were right, Hart." Regret glimmered in her pretty blue eyes. "I have been hiding out here, delaying my return to a normal life."

Shoving his fingers through his hair, he tamped down the need to pull her into his arms and kiss her again. "I'm beginning to think I should keep my big mouth shut," he grumbled.

She laughed, as he meant her to, then lifted her hands in wordless surrender. "Look. I—"

"Need to think about it?" he guessed.

Maggie squared her slender shoulders. "Give me a night to sleep on it. At the very least."

"I DON'T SEE what the problem is, especially if Mr. Sexy heads back to California," Callie said, an hour later, when Maggie had filled her in. "You needed time to find another job, and make a concrete plan, and this will certainly give you that."

Maggie paced the length of her office. "The problem is I'll still be caught up in everything with his family."

"So what's different about that?" Callie countered. "You've been caught up all along."

"Yes, but Hart—and his baby—weren't part of that. Now, they are." And it made the situation so much more emotionally treacherous.

Callie paused. "Have you been kissing him?"

Maggie gasped. Glad her sister wasn't there to see her blush, she chided, "Callie!"

"Look, I'm all for you jumping back into love."

"No one's talking about love." The attraction between her and Hart was pure budding friendship with the potential for sex. There was a difference.

"Look, I know there are those in our family that do not agree, but I don't think you have to live the life of a cloistered nun."

Maggie scoffed. "I don't know how you can say that, when that's exactly what you've been doing. At least you have been since you became a widow."

Callie harrumphed. "And that is a story for

another day. We're talking about you here, Maggie. And the fact that I think you should do whatever you need to do to be happy. Which should be easier than ever, now that Gus is finally moving on, too."

Maggie let another chunk of the massive guilt she'd been carrying for the last couple of years go. She kicked off her shoes, picked up her iPad and stretched out on the office sofa. "I heard via the Laramie grapevine that he's serious about someone."

"Nancy Lindholm. Rumor is, they're going to get married."

"Then why," she asked slowly, looking at the message that had just popped up on her screen, "is he suddenly emailing me? Especially, after all this time?"

HART WOKE TO the sound of a loud, piercing wail at two-thirty in the morning. "Mommy!" Henry cried. "Mommy!"

Adrenaline kicked in. He plucked Henry out

of the crib, his heart going out to his son. "It's okay." Hart patted him on the back, just as he had earlier in the day, reassuring. "Your dad's here."

"Mommy! Mommy!" Henry repeated, wailing even louder.

Seconds later, Maggie appeared in the doorway, looking just as concerned. She was clad in a pair of floral-print pajama pants and a scoopneck white cotton T-shirt that nicely outlined her slender body. Her dark hair was tousled, her cheeks pink with sleep. "What do you need?" she mouthed.

"Mommy!' Henry cried again, even more hysterically. He held his little arms out to Maggie. "Mommy. Mommy. Mommy…"

The ache in his son's voice echoed deep in Hart's soul. Henry continued reaching for Maggie. Wordlessly, she closed the distance between them, took Henry and snuggled him against her chest with a tenderness that made something raw and elemental twist in Hart's gut.

"It's all right, sweetheart," she said softly, her voice suddenly thick with tears, too. "You're all right."

At the magically soothing sound of her voice, Henry's head dropped onto her shoulder. His eyes shut. His breathing became deep and even once again.

"Nightmare?" Hart mused.

Maggie continued to walk Henry back and forth. Her expression contained the relief Hart felt. "Probably." She checked the baby's diaper. "He's a little wet, too."

Hart grabbed a clean diaper and brought it over. Maggie started to hand Henry over to Hart for changing, but the little boy clung tight.

Hart felt a mixture of frustration and hurt he knew he had no right to feel. After all, he hadn't been there for his son. Hadn't even known Henry existed until now.

Misreading the reason behind his silence, Maggie asked kindly, "Want me to try?"

Hart nodded, his heart in his throat.

Maggie laid Henry down gently in his crib. When he started to whimper again, she soothed him with quiet words and a gentle touch. Swiftly, she finished and lifted him right back into her arms.

"Now what?" Hart asked, aware all over again just how little he knew about taking care of a baby. Or a kid of any age, for that matter.

Maggie smiled and pressed a kiss into the top of Henry's head. "A bottle of warm milk should do the trick."

"I'll get it." Hart went downstairs.

When he returned, Maggie was sitting in the rocking chair, Henry cuddled on her lap. "I can take over from here," Hart said.

Looking a little disappointed, Maggie rose. She attempted to hand Henry to Hart, only to have Henry let out a primal scream that indicated what the toddler thought of the idea.

"Mind hanging out here a few minutes longer?" Hart asked with a heavy sigh.

Maggie settled back into the rocking chair. "No problem."

Hart handed the bottle over. Henry relaxed contentedly in Maggie's arms while she rocked.

A blissful silence fell.

Maggie turned her glance to his. "I wonder if Henry has any loveys," she said softly.

"Loveys?" He stared at her in confusion.

"A favorite blanket. Or toy that he uses to soothe himself."

Hart mentally inventoried the belongings in the diaper bag and lone suitcase that had been sent with his son. "I didn't see anything like that."

Maggie accepted that information with a nod. Taking charge once again, she asked, "Then how would you feel about going to get some tomorrow?"

"I DON'T THINK he's going to be able to choose just one," Maggie told Hart the next morning in the aisle of the San Antonio baby superstore.

Hart shrugged, aware this was a lot more fun than he had anticipated, especially given he wasn't a guy who liked shopping. "Then let's get all of them."

Maggie made a face. "We're talking about seven stuffed animals," she cautioned.

"A boy needs his toys," Hart declared. "Besides, it's not like they're going to take up an enormous amount of room in a suitcase. They're only seven or eight inches long each." And all soft and cuddly as could be. Just like Maggie in her pajamas, fresh out of bed.

Not that he'd had the chance to experience that firsthand, other than visually.

Still, he knew the memory would stick with him.

Oblivious of the direction of his thoughts, Maggie steered them down the health aisle. "We also need a first aid kit for babies, and an ear thermometer because those are much easier to use."

They shopped on, adding a booster-seat-style

high chair that could easily be attached to any regular table chair. "What else?" Hart asked, after they had added a package of toddler bath toys.

Maggie gave him a cautious look. "I went through the clothing in the suitcase this morning before we left. A lot of it was awfully small."

Hart had noticed his son's clothes were kind of snug, too. He hadn't been sure if that was the way they were supposed to fit or not. "I'm guessing he needs a bigger size."

Together, they selected a dozen T-shirts, shorts, pajamas, socks and a new pair of better fitting shoes. She not only easily found what they needed, she steered him to the best-wearing brands. "We want you to get your money's worth."

Yet another thing to admire about her. "How do you know all this?" he asked her casually. "Is it because you were a nanny?"

She nodded. "Plus, I've helped Callie shop

for her son. And I also spearheaded the baby shower for her when she was pregnant with Brian."

He caught the brief, wistful look in her eyes and sensed she might need to talk about it. "Was that difficult for you, having your twin sister pregnant when you weren't?"

Maggie sighed and cast a fond look at his son. "It was a little bit hard, at times." She paused to ruffle Henry's hair, then turned back to Hart. "We'd always done everything together, and we'd always figured we would have our children around the same time and bring them up together."

Aware the cart was getting a little full—and probably heavy, too—Hart stepped in to push it forward. "How old is her son?"

They continued on down the aisle, his steps small enough to accommodate hers. "A little over a year," Maggie allowed. "Sadly, she lost her husband, Seth, before Brian was born. So her little boy never got to meet his dad."

Hart touched her shoulder briefly. "I'm sorry to hear that."

"Yeah. He was a great guy. Callie's been a real trouper, though. And of course, she has her son, who is absolutely adorable...." Her voice trailed off wistfully.

He admired the glossy sheen of her dark brown hair. "Are you close to him?"

"Yes," she said softly, coming abruptly, intimately close, "but to be clear, I've never met a baby I didn't fall immediately in love with."

He inhaled her hyacinth perfume. "Including Henry."

Maggie sighed and looked even more wistful. "Even and especially Henry. But not to worry. I know how to love from a distance, too." She leaned over and gently bussed Henry's forehead. "So, I won't forget you when you head off to California, little man."

Henry beamed up at her, elated by the feminine attention, and chattered happily.

But will you forget me? Hart wondered. Then

immediately pushed the thought away. He and Maggie were little more than friends who had shared one kiss. And unless she changed her plans and was open to at least visiting him in California, friends were all they would likely be.

Having tired of sitting in the basket, Henry started squirming and reached for Maggie. Appearing happy for the distraction, she undid the safety strap and lifted the little boy out of the shopping basket. A stuffed animal in each hand, he snuggled against her. Hart couldn't help but note that Maggie looked just as contented.

"Now, where are the blankets?" she asked. "We need to get a few of those, too, to use as loveys. Preferably in the same color and size, so if one is being laundered—"

"Another can take its place," Hart interjected wisely, wondering when his son would warm up to him as much as he had to Maggie.

Maggie winked. "You catch on fast."

She turned her attention back to Henry and playfully pretended to zoom Henry over to Hart. Then, at the very last minute, teasingly snatched him back again. Henry giggled. Maggie did it again. Hart did his part, hamming up his surprise when he almost got to hold the little boy, his deflation when he did not. And on they went, with Henry giggling more infectiously each time. By the time Maggie actually put Henry in Hart's arms, Henry was more than happy to go.

Hart sent her a grateful glance. He didn't know what he would have done without her the last twenty-four hours. He was glad he hadn't had to find out. "You make this easy."

Maggie patted his biceps, all business once again. "It's going to get even easier," she told him sincerely. "You'll see."

HART HAD FIGURED they were done. Or close to it. Not so. There were many other items, big and small, that Henry needed—including child safety gates, and a baby monitor with multiple receivers—so it was another hour or so before they left the baby superstore. By then, everyone was hungry, so they stopped at a popular chain restaurant. Henry seemed very comfortable in the brightly lit environment. He did not mind sitting in the high chair and really chowed down on the chicken strips, French fries and applesauce.

In fact, he was enjoying himself so much that Maggie and Hart lingered after they had finished their own meals and ordered coffees for themselves.

Hart affectionately watched Henry dip another French fry in the sauce, then turned that same affection back to her. "That shirt is going to be covered in ketchup," he observed, with a shake of his handsome head.

At last, a problem she could easily solve. Maggie placed her elbow on the table and propped her chin on her upraised fist. "That's why we bought that spray-on prewash stain remover. Because he's a boy and boys are messy."

Hart pretended to take affront. He shifted. Beneath the table, their knees touched. "How would you know?" he teased. "You're a girl."

Maggie bragged, "I've also been around boys all my life."

He chuckled, then gave her the leisurely once-over. "That's usually the case with pretty girls."

Maggie felt herself flush at his thoroughly male attention. "How do you know I was pretty growing up?"

Hunger appeared in his eyes. "You can't look like you do today and not have been a real looker in your younger days." She had the strangest sensation that he was thinking about kissing her again. Would have, had they been anywhere else.

Suddenly, her phone beeped to let her know a call was coming in. Grateful for the interruption, she switched screens and glanced at the caller ID.

Maggie looked at Hart. "It's your folks." Then she put the phone to her ear and answered. "Hey. What's up?"

It was business first, as usual. Then Fiona Sanders got around to the real reason she was calling. "So my question is, can you continue to help Hart with our grandson until we can get home?"

Maggie knew this was as critical to her employers as any business deal. "Yes," she said. "Absolutely."

"Good. Because although he can take a steam engine apart and rebuild it, he knows nothing about taking care of children."

That was a little unfair. "He's a quick study," Maggie found herself defending him, a little emotionally.

Fiona paused. "Well, there is that. Unfortunately, cutting our cruise short and rearranging our travel plans proved to be both impossible and hideously expensive, so we won't be home any earlier than scheduled. In the meantime, would you be a doll and send us a photo or two of daddy and son?"

"I will," Maggie promised.

Maggie hung up and reset her phone. "Mind moving over there next to Henry so I can take your picture?"

"You're kidding, right?"

"Nope. This is a moment your mother and father want to remember."

Hart looked horrified. "Henry's covered with ketchup."

Maggie grinned. "Even better. An action photo."

He guffawed and complied. Maggie showed Hart the shot, then quickly texted the photo to his folks. Henry indicated he was finished. Maggie tore open one of the cleanup cloths the server had thoughtfully provided. She began the process of cleaning the little boy up the best she could.

"So, why did my parents call you?" Hart handed over his credit card, to pay the bill.

"They wanted to let me know that the Jaworskis talked to them after they talked to me. And they've decided to bring their daughter, her fiancé, members of the groom's family and sundry other members of their wedding party back out to the ranch tomorrow morning, at ten, to ride the train to Nature's Cathedral and have another look."

"Sounds promising."

"I hope so." The wedding was going to be so large. It would mean a lot to the ranch's bottom line to get that booking.

"What else?"

Maggie undid a squirming Henry's safety belt and lifted him out of the chair while filling Hart in on the rest of what had been said. "And of course they wanted my promise that I would continue to help you out with Henry until they could get back." And she was happy to do that, provided she did not get too emotionally involved with his handsome, charming daddy in the process.

THE REST OF the day went quickly. Henry slept in the car on the drive back from San Antonio. Hart took him out for a walk around the gardens when they got back, while Maggie went into the office and caught up on everything that absolutely had to be done. Then she took over for Hart, who had his own phone calls to make.

Hart looked grim when he came out of the office.

He walked wordlessly over to say hello to his son, who was seated on a soft cotton rug Maggie had placed in front of the bay window in the adjacent breakfast room. Hart enjoyed Henry's spirited demonstration, banging plastic bowls and serving spoons. He kissed the top of his head, then walked over to join Maggie in the kitchen. "Everything all right?" she asked, looking up from the steamed zucchini and squash she was preparing on the stove.

Hart's expression remained maddeningly inscrutable. "Just the usual chaos when someone on the security team has an unexpected absence."

Except Hart wasn't just someone on Monica Day's team—he was the head of the star's personal security detail. And Monica had an overseas tour coming up shortly.

Feeling oddly threatened, Maggie asked lightly, "Are they going to be able to survive without you?"

His eyes turned even darker. "It's my job to see that they do."

Outside, a car approached the house. Then stopped. A door slammed.

Hart moved to the window that overlooked the parking area at the rear of the detached garage. His brow furrowed. "Expecting someone?"

Now? Maggie frowned. "No. Why?"

Hart pointed to the person coming up the walk. "I think this gentleman's here for you."

Chapter Six

Maggie stared at her ex-fiancé in surprise, aware Gus Radcliffe looked better than the last time she had seen him two years ago. Like he had been working out regularly. His clothes were neat and polished, too.

Whereas she was clad in a blouse with a smear of orange Popsicle on the shoulder and walking shorts with a blotch of ketchup on the hip. All remnants of Henry's day. And hers. Not that she minded. Except…she didn't want any of this getting back to Laramie. And the rest of the McCabes.

"Gus? What are you doing here?"

He looked at her imploringly. "Callie said that if I was going to have this conversation with you, I needed to do it face-to-face."

Aware it was pretty hot outside, Maggie ushered him into air conditioned comfort.

Henry ran after her. "Mommy, Mommy." He grabbed at the hem of Maggie's shorts, then lifted his hands to be picked up.

Gus looked at Maggie in surprise.

She shook her head and lifted a hand to signal all was not as it seemed, and saw Gus relax in return.

Luckily for Maggie, Hart was right behind them. His expression pleasant but indecipherable, he nodded briefly at Gus, then said, "I've got this."

Playfully, Hart scooped Henry up in his arms. "Let's go check out your new toys, okay, fella? We'll be in the living room if you need us." He departed, his son still babbling happily.

Maggie and Gus were left standing there alone. Maggie wished she'd had more warning, especially since her ex's expression was as stressed out as his voice.

"Why didn't you answer my email?" he asked.

Maggie poured iced tea. "I haven't heard from you in two years, and you suddenly want to know if we could get together for dinner sometime this weekend? In Laramie, of all places. What did you expect me to say?"

Gus sprinkled a little artificial sweetener in his drink. "Okay, maybe that wasn't the best place for us to meet."

"Given how much interest there would be in seeing the two of us together again, probably not. Besides, I heard through the grapevine you were dating someone. Pretty seriously, as a matter of fact."

"I am."

Maggie held her glass in front of her like a shield. "Then…?"

Gus slumped against the counter. "Nancy

found out what happened on our wedding day. She wants to talk to you before she'll accept my proposal."

"You've been awfully quiet this evening. Is everything okay?" Hart asked, hours later, after rocking Henry to sleep. He came into the room and switched on one of the baby monitor transmitters now in every major room of the ranch house. The staticky silence indicated that Henry was still asleep. Which meant the two of them could relax.

Maggie was sitting on the living room sofa, taking the tags off the stacks of Henry's new clothes. "I just have a lot on my mind."

Hart sat down on the other end of the sofa. "Gus?"

Feeling powerless against the all-encompassing intensity of his gaze, Maggie batted her lashes. "Why, Hart Sanders, if I didn't know better," she drawled, pausing to lay a hand across her chest in true Texas-belle fashion, "I'd think you were feeling jealous."

"Is there a reason for me to be?" he asked cheerfully.

Much more of this and she'd end up pouring her heart out to him. "No." She dropped tags into the pile on the coffee table.

"So, the two of you are just friends?"

Deciding this was a road she did not want to go down, Maggie reached for another cute little shirt. "What is it about baby clothes that make you want a baby…?" she murmured.

"Maybe the baby you're buying them for?" Briefly, his hand covered hers. He waited until she met his gaze before he continued, "And you didn't answer my question. Is there something going on between you and Gus that I should be aware of?"

Was he jealous or just cautious about cutting in on some other man's territory? Maggie didn't want to think what either option might mean.

She swallowed. Carefully aligning the scissors between cloth and tag, she cut another plastic string. "If you must know," and it appeared that he did, "here's a fun fact. With the exception of this evening, Gus and I haven't spoken directly to each other since the day after the wedding that wasn't."

Hart picked up a stack and began ripping off the impossibly stubborn tags—with his bare hands. All without hurting a single garment. "You're still angry with him for whatever he said to you following the rehearsal dinner?"

Aware Hart wouldn't rest until he had an answer, Maggie paused. "Not angry, exactly. I'm just relieved we didn't get married. Gus and I would have been all wrong for each other."

Hart finished his task, then shifted the stack between them to the coffee table. He moved so he was sitting right next to her, one arm draped across the back of the sofa. Not quite touching her, but close enough she could feel his body heat. He searched her eyes. "So you're saying he doesn't want you back?"

Maggie reached for the last stack of clothing and put it on her lap. Finding Hart's scrutiny way too unnerving, she ducked her head as she went back to the task. "He's trying to get engaged to Nancy Lindholm."

"What do you mean—trying?"

Deciding she needed to get this over with as quickly as possible, Maggie set the clothes aside. She turned to face Hart directly. "Apparently, Nancy won't say yes to Gus unless she talks to me first."

Hart's brows knit together. "That's…odd."

Tell me about it. "She's worried that whatever made me run away from him on my wedding day is cause for concern for her, too."

Hart paused. "Why did you run?"

Maggie reminded herself that discretion was the better part of valor. Plus, the classy thing to do after any breakup was to say as little as possible—to everyone. "Gus and I made a pact not to talk about that with anyone."

"And yet here he is." Hart's gaze held her eyes sagely. "Asking you to what, exactly?"

Maggie released an uneven breath. "Tell her it's okay to marry him, without telling her why I didn't."

Hart reached over and took her hand, the gesture both comforting and seductive. "I'm guessing Ms. Lindholm doesn't know about your argument with Gus after the rehearsal dinner?"

"No one knows. Except the two of us, and well, you because of what you overheard in the woods that day."

He narrowed his gaze. "You didn't tell *anyone?*"

Maggie flushed. "No."

Hart smoothed his thumb across the top of her hand, lightly tracing the veins. "Not even Callie?"

Maggie shrugged and forced herself to focus

on Hart's face rather than what his touch was doing to her. "She was busy being a blissful newlywed. I didn't want to ruin that time for her by going on and on about my issues. Then, a few months later, Seth died in that car accident, right after she found out she was pregnant, and I knew it would be wrong to burden her with that then."

Hart let her go and sat back against the cushions. "Surely, you could have talked to one of your other sisters."

Maggie had considered it. Any one of them would have understood. She rose and carried the stacks of clothes to the laundry room. "I decided not to do that, either."

He followed lazily. "Why not?"

Knowing it was best to launder a child's new clothing before wearing, to remove any irritants in the fabric, Maggie sorted them by color, dropping the dark clothing into the laundry first.

"Because at the time it was too upsetting,

and after the dust settled, our relationship was over, so it no longer mattered. Hence, the classy thing to do was to spare our families any more gossip. Remain silent. And keep what should remain private, private."

Hart lounged against the dryer, arms folded in front of him, watching. "Except that it's still bothering you."

Maggie added baby detergent, switched on the washer and closed the lid. She turned to face Hart. "You're suggesting I tell you?"

"I've already heard half of it."

He had a point. She'd carried this around for too long.

"I think I might have mentioned how caught up Callie and I both were in the planning of our double wedding. What I didn't talk about were the doubts I kept having."

Maggie met his eyes. The look of understanding on his handsome face gave her the courage to go on. "I think I knew almost from the moment the engagement ring was on my finger that Gus and I hadn't so much decided to get married, as fallen into it—mostly because we were already living together and marriage seemed like the next logical step."

"Like this was just the way your life was supposed to go," he intuited.

She nodded, already beginning to feel better. "Maybe if we'd let down our guards enough to talk honestly and realistically about what our expectations were, we would have realized early on that we weren't nearly as well-matched as we thought."

"But you didn't."

Maggie put the clothes still needing to be laundered into a basket, then went back to lean against the washer. "Gus isn't a particularly social guy, so he stayed as far away from all the wedding commotion as possible, while I concentrated on the upcoming nuptials."

Hart came to stand beside her once again. Tilting her head back to look up at him, she forced herself to go on with her account. "Had

Gus not asked me to go for one last moon-lit walk the night before our wedding, said he would be glad when it was all over and he would no longer have to see so much family, I never would have known how differently we felt. Turns out, Gus had always privately re-sented having to spend so much time with my family—and now that we were getting mar-ried, his—but the year of living in the same house with my twin sister and her beau as we prepared for the wedding had really pushed him over the edge. To the point he wanted us to look for jobs and move to another state. Pref-erably one as far away as possible."

Hart regarded her with a mixture of shock and sympathy.

Comforted, Maggie continued, "And if we stayed in Texas after the wedding, he expected me to scale way back on any time I spent with Callie and only see our respective kin once or twice a year."

Hart took her by the hand and led her back

to the living room. "I'm guessing that's not how you saw your future shaping up." As they moved through the hall, he wrapped a comforting hand around her waist.

"Connection with family is everything to me. Loving and caring for each other is what being a McCabe is all about."

They sat on the sofa, side by side, their bodies touching. "So why didn't you call it off, then?" Hart asked.

Maggie let herself snuggle in the curve of his arm. "Because Gus saw how upset I was and said of course we didn't have to move if I didn't want to, and that we would work out a compromise when we got back from the honeymoon."

Hart studied her. "Were you okay with that?"

"Not really, because once he told me how he really felt I saw that it was always going to be an issue between us."

"But?"

"I just couldn't wrap my mind around the

thought of calling anything off at that point, after the months of planning and all the money and time that had been spent." She traced the hem of her walking shorts and continued miserably, "Plus, remember, we had four hundred guests in San Antonio hotels that were being transported out to the ranch for the mountain-top ceremony."

Hart grimaced in a way that let her know he did remember what an enormous undertaking that day had been, in many respects. From the dozens of flowers to the top-notch society caterers, to the string orchestra on the mountain-top, her parents and those of Gus and Seth had spared no expense.

Maggie sighed. "Anyway, I accepted his apology and we made up. And I went on to bed, determined to put our argument behind us. But I couldn't sleep at all that night. I kept thinking about what Gus had said, and wondering what *would* happen if Gus and I cancelled our part of the double wedding. Until I finally realized, around dawn, I would be more relieved than sad, and that worried me even more."

"So why didn't you bow out of it—at that point?" Hart asked curiously.

Maggie winced. "Because I still didn't want to accept that I'd made a mistake of that enormity. Plus," Maggie shrugged, "there were our families. And Callie and her happiness. I didn't want to ruin anything for her."

Maggie stood, began to pace.

"And it really was, by all standards of decency, too late to make it a single wedding instead of a double wedding ceremony." She knit her hands in front of her. "So I convinced myself it was just the pre-wedding jitters for both of us, and everything would be all right once Gus and I were married."

His gaze reflective, Hart joined her at the mantle. "But when you were walking down the aisle on your dad's arm—"

Maggie flushed, embarrassed but not really

surprised. She'd felt the sensuality of Hart's appraisal, even then. "You saw that?"

"I noticed everything about you that day. I couldn't take my eyes off of you." He caught her hand and brought it to his lips for a soft, sincere kiss. "You were, without a doubt, the most beautiful bride I had ever seen in my life."

HART DIDN'T NEED to see Maggie draw in a quick breath of surprise, form a ghost of a smile and then fall awkwardly silent to know he had just given away too much. She'd barely recovered from her last relationship. She sure wasn't ready for another. Nor was he, given that he had just found out he was a daddy and was still struggling to learn how to care for his son. But there was definitely an attraction there, one he hoped to act on when the time was right.

In the meantime, he needed to slow down. At least a little bit. He flashed an encouraging smile, then prodded casually, "Back to what you were thinking during your walk down the aisle?"

Her face lost its color as she began to reflect. "My anxiety got worse with every step I took. I kept telling myself to just get through the ceremony, that we could sort it all out later—quietly and privately—if I still felt panicked."

"Hire a lawyer—" Hart guessed.

Maggie nodded. "And use the fact we hadn't so much as consummated our marriage or gone on a honeymoon to end our union as quickly and painlessly as possible."

"And for a moment you thought you could manage that," he guessed.

"But when it finally came time to take him as my husband, I just couldn't do it. Not knowing how he felt about family in general, and mine in particular. So, I ran, figuring as embarrassing and upsetting as that was, it was still better than having to go through the expense and embarrassment of a divorce, on top of everything else."

The pain in her voice made him want to reassure her, so Hart took her in his arms. Savoring her warmth and her femininity, he gently stroked a hand through her hair. "You did the right thing."

She leaned her head against his shoulder. "That's easy for you to say. I didn't do the honorable thing a whole lot earlier and leave *you* standing at the altar."

"And you wouldn't, either," Hart told her gruffly.

Maggie whirled away from him. "Why? Because you wouldn't ask me to marry you in the first place?"

"Because," he returned softly, "it would never come to that."

"Sure it would," she countered, revealing even more of her private pain. "Haven't you heard?" Suddenly, tears sparkled in her eyes. "I'm damaged goods. Or in other words, not worth betting on."

He stepped closer, and before she could

run, cupped her shoulders warmly. "The heck you're not."

Color came back into her face. She tipped her chin defiantly.

"Stop hiding behind the past, Maggie," he told her before she could protest any more. "Stop hiding behind your mistakes."

"THAT'S NOT WHAT I'm doing!" Maggie declared, doing her best to remain imperious.

Not an easy task when her whole body was zinging from the protective feel of his hands on her shoulders and Hart was standing in front of her like a conquering hero, ready to rescue her as surely as he had that day in the woods.

"Sure, it is." He offered her his killer smile and gave her the lazy once-over before returning ever so deliberately to her lips. He paused to look deep into her eyes. "You think if you don't ever let yourself get involved with anyone again, you'll never be hurt again."

He was so on target with his assessment she felt her knees buckle, just a tad. Determined not to let him know how much he was getting under her skin, Maggie huffed, "So what do you suggest I do to get out of this rut I'm in?" Even though, deep inside, the woman in her already knew.

Hart delivered a slow, heart-stopping smile. "This."

Before she could draw a breath, he cupped her face in both hands, lowered his lips to hers and delivered the most tantalizing kiss she'd ever experienced in her life.

Maggie hadn't been prepared for *that,* and she moaned as he deepened the connection, his body pressing up against hers, his tongue mingling with hers, the pleasurable caress wreaking havoc with her carefully built defenses.

She hadn't realized—until now—just how much she needed to be loved. Hadn't realized just how lonely she had felt until he walked back into her life.

She broke off the kiss and let her forehead fall to his shoulders. She knew this was crazy, especially since Hart Sanders had unwittingly—and unknowingly—fueled her fantasies the last two years.

Swallowing, she regarded him closely. "Are you rescuing me again?"

His eyes were dark and unwavering on hers. He rubbed his thumb across her lower lip. "A little bit," he said softly. "But only," he dipped his head, "because you seem to need it."

He kissed her again. Sensation swept through her, more potent than before. And suddenly, everything she'd held back came pouring forth. Everything she wanted rose to the surface. And what she wanted most, Maggie conceded silently, was Hart.

"You mean that?" she asked.

Chuckling, he dropped a string of kisses

down the nape of her neck, across her cheek, up her jaw, then hovered over her lips. "I do."

Maggie trembled at the raw tenderness in his gaze.

Appearing to like what he saw, he smiled and kissed her again, even more provocatively this time.

Passion roared through her, sudden and fierce as a summer storm. Maggie flattened her palms across the front of his shirt. He slid his palms down her spine, rested them on her hips, pressed her lower half to his. She surged against him, knowing it was foolish and short-sighted, yet wanting to deepen the connection between them so badly. To find something, anything, that would keep him from walking away.

And still they kissed. And kissed. And kissed. Until their hearts pounded in unison and she couldn't think of any place else she would rather be. He was hot and hard and male.

And he wanted her as much as she wanted him. "Upstairs," she whispered.

She didn't have to ask twice. He lifted her in his arms and carried her, still kissing her, all the way to her bed. He set her down gently. "You're sure?"

Already unbuttoning her blouse, Maggie nodded. "I'm okay with just sex." She was strong enough to handle what could only be a very temporary thing. Besides, he couldn't break her heart unless she let him. And she wasn't going to let him. All she was going to do was lose herself in a very passionate, very physical interlude. Once.

He studied her carefully. "I'm not sure I believe that."

She dropped her blouse to the floor, unhooked her bra. "Believe it."

His gaze moved over the soft curves of her breasts and her taut pink nipples. He inhaled a jerky breath.

She let her shorts follow. Then her panties.

Fierce satisfaction and longing glimmered in his dark brown eyes. Smiling, he reached for her, "Against my better judgment, I'm beginning to."

She held him at bay, hand to his chest. "Uh-huh. You, too."

He grinned, complied and slowly reeled her in. "Bossy, aren't you?"

She answered his mischievous look with one of her own. "You're about to find out just how much."

Liking the challenge, he kicked his clothes out of the way. She pressed against him, savoring the brisk masculine fragrance of his hair and skin. As they kissed, she explored his broad shoulders, nicely sculpted chest, flat abs and lower still…well, she decided, that was awfully nice, too.

He did his part, as well, deepening the connection, parting her lips with his, kissing her until passion and need shot through her like flames. He threaded a hand through her hair, cupped the back of her neck and leaned in, taking everything, even as he gave. Until she was gasping for breath, her entire body liquefying with every gentle masterful stroke of his tongue. He shifted her against a wall and slid a knee between her thighs. She moved her weight onto it and discovered a whole new way of giving and getting pleasure.

She whimpered against him in frustration, the friction of their bodies not nearly enough. He murmured her name in a silky soft whisper, and then she was straining all the more, her body abruptly finding the escape she'd been wanting.

He grinned against her lips and said her name again as her shudders subsided. The next thing she knew, she was lying on her bed and he was stretched out beside her. He draped a leg across her thighs, holding her still, as he plundered her mouth again and again. Her hips arched to try to meet his, but he held her still, simultaneously raising her heart rate and slowing them down. Making her realize how long and how badly she had wanted not just to walk on the wild side, but with him. Wanted hot, mind-blowing, totally irrational sex. With a hot, mesmerizing, mystifying hero of a man.

She'd finally found him. Only he wasn't co-operating. She broke off the kiss long enough to say, "Can we speed this up a little?"

Laughter rumbled deep in his chest. "No."

She let out a muffled sound of disappointment—not really all that surprised. After all, she'd learned that day in the woods, he liked to do things his way, too.

His mouth slid over the nape of her neck, his teeth scraping the skin, causing an erotic little shiver. "We're going to make this last." He cupped her breasts, his thumbs rubbing the nipples into aching buds of arousal. "And don't worry," he winked, "you'll thank me later."

Lost in the pleasure, she shut her eyes and let her head fall back, giving him even greater access. She kissed the side of his neck, his temple, hoping to change his mind. "I'm going out of my mind right now."

"Good." He found his way to her mouth again, paused to search her face for only he knew what. Irises darkening, he kissed her again, slowly and completely ravishing her. "It'll make it all that much better when you come."

She was about to come now. Again. All on account of his kiss. She moaned, letting him know just that.

"Patience," he whispered, his eyes serious now. Grasping both her wrists in one hand, he kissed his way down to her breasts, languidly exploring her nipples. She was hopelessly aroused, impatient.

"Too much?" he murmured, finding his way back to her lips.

She gasped when he caught her up against his hard, warm body. "Just right." She let her hands slide down his sides, to his hips. "Except..." she whispered back as her heart tripped, "I want you in me."

Hart grinned. "We can work on that."

He lowered his head and kissed her senseless, and only when she'd arched against him, did he continue his quest. Moving lower, more intimately still. Until her skin felt so hot it almost sizzled and it was everything she could do to keep her spiraling feelings in check.

And then he was sliding up, taking her all the way in his arms. Wanting fulfillment to go both ways, she shifted, so he was beneath her. And then she did the same for him, until there was no more waiting, no more holding back, and he was over the top of her once again. Easing his hands beneath her, he lifted her. Her muscles trembled, tensed, as he settled between her thighs once again, his hips nudging hers apart.

He took her slowly and masterfully. Allowing her the time to adjust to the weight and size of him, then going deeper still, until there was no more thinking. Only feeling and the inevitable build of passion and sensation that ended with her falling apart in his arms.

For a moment, they hung together suspended in incredible pleasure. Maggie closed her eyes and cuddled close, savoring his warmth and strength. The slow, eventual drift back to reality followed. And with that, the sudden realization that maybe she wasn't as completely in control as she ought to be.

With effort, Maggie forced herself to extricate herself from his sensual hold. She didn't want to shake off the delicious feeling of well-being that came from such an earth-shattering release. But she knew to stay would tempt her to make this into something more than the pure physical awakening that it was.

She had done that once.

Let herself fall casually into something out of ease and convenience—only to find herself trapped in a web of her own making.

She was definitely not doing it again.

HART FELT MAGGIE remove herself emotionally from their embrace, long before she moved away physically. He had sensed this was coming. Maggie wasn't the kind of woman who let anyone in. Even when she had been engaged to Gus, she had all but admitted she'd had a wall around her heart. A wall that had gotten stronger and higher over time. Kept in place for all sorts of reasons, the least of which was pride.

Maggie shimmied into her tiny yellow panties and then eased on the matching silk bra. "Why are you looking at me?"

He sighed luxuriantly, his body already ready for more, just as he suspected she was, if the tightening of her nipples was any indication. "Just wondering."

She turned, hands on her hips, her shiny brown hair spilling over her shoulders in erotic disarray.

"Did I say or do something to make you want to cut this short?"

She wrinkled her nose, mischief in her pretty blue eyes. "Besides that little moan…at the very end…?"

He grinned at her teasing. Then waited, really wanting and needing to know.

"No," she admitted on a disgruntled exhalation of breath when he still refused to let her off the hook. "You didn't say or do anything."

"Then why are you over there, getting dressed?" He patted the mattress beside him playfully, still hopeful she'd come to her senses. "When you should still be here, with me."

Maggie bent to pick up her shirt and put her arms through the sleeves. "Because Henry could be up in the middle of the night tonight."

Hart hoped not. Although as an ex-nanny, she probably knew what was she was talking about.

"You should sleep while you can," she advised with a brisk smile, slipping on her shorts.

Sleep wasn't what he wanted, and they both knew it.

However, it seemed she had made up her mind—that making love once was enough for her—so he reluctantly remained where he was. Maggie got down on her hands and knees and rummaged around for her socks and sneakers, two of which seemed to have landed under the bed. "And tomorrow's going to be a long day for me. The Jaworskis are coming at ten, and I want to be at my best."

Hart swung his legs over the bed, and reached for his boxers. He wanted this to end well, and he sensed it would go better if he were dressed, too. "Think it will all go okay?" he asked casually.

She surreptitiously watched him pull on his boxers. When he caught her admiring his physique, a faint blush highlighted her cheeks. "I hope so."

Glad she wasn't as immune as she pretended, he crossed to her side. "Anything else before you go?"

She splayed her hands across his chest, her palms ghosting across his nipples, before coming to rest on his pecs. "This was nice." She stood on tiptoe and brushed a brief kiss across his mouth. "But we really can't do this again."

Chapter Seven

At eight the next morning, Maggie paused just outside the kitchen, on the other side of the newly installed child-safety gate. She was dressed for work, but Hart was still in loose-fitting plaid pajama pants and a short-sleeved gray T-shirt. Thick sandy brown hair rumpled and standing on end, the morning beard stubbling his handsome face, he looked a little ragged around the edges.

Henry, on the other hand, was wide awake and already dressed in jeans and a T-shirt. He was sitting on the soft cotton rug beneath the bay window, playing with his array of stuffed animals and toys.

His dad was standing at the stove, stirring something and waiting for the coffee to finish brewing. He turned and took her in, his expression warm and welcoming.

A tingle of awareness swept through her. Maggie smiled and hiked up her knee length skirt just enough to step over the child safety gate. "Rough night?"

Hart handed over a plate of applewood-smoked bacon and waited while she helped herself to a perfectly crisped slice. "You heard us?"

"A little," she fibbed, pretending she hadn't been laying there, listening to every soothing word and baby gurgle. The sweet intimacy of the moment had beckoned her. "But you seemed to be handling it just fine, and I know the two of you need to bond, sooner rather than later, so…" She'd resisted the urge to join in the nighttime activity and instead had stayed in bed.

Hart put two pieces of bread in the toaster and pushed the lever down. "I won't pretend we didn't miss you, but the time alone together did seem to do something to bring us closer together." Grinning, he poured coffee for both of them and then came nearer. "Even if it deprived us both of some much-needed sleep."

Maggie smelled the fragrances of minty toothpaste, sleep and man. She pushed aside the sensual memories of their time together, and for all of their sakes, moved back slightly. "Any idea why he was awake so much?"

Their hands touched as Hart handed her a mug. Remembering how she liked it, he got out the vanilla-flavored creamer and handed it to her. "He wanted to play with all his new stuffed animals."

Maggie blinked. "You put them *all* in there with him?"

Hart's sexy grin widened and laugh lines appeared at the corners of his eyes. "I tried giving him just one at a time, but he let me know he wanted them all in there. And when that happened, it was party central."

Maggie chuckled, easily able to envision the happy daddy-son scene. "So what time did Henry finally go back to sleep?" As if she didn't already know!

"I think I finally rocked him back to dreamland about five a.m."

And they'd gotten up at seven-thirty, Maggie knew. Right before she slipped out of bed and headed for her own shower. She looked over at the happy toddler, who was busy dramatically acting out a babbling nonsensical conversation between elephant and tiger. "Well, Henry doesn't seem to be the worse for wear." Maggie went over to the rug and knelt down beside him. "You're surprisingly full of energy, aren't you, little guy?"

Understanding the question had been posed

to him, Henry picked up a giraffe and handed it to Maggie.

She accepted it with a hug and a kiss. "Well, thank you, Henry."

He gave her a pat on the shoulder in return, then took the giraffe back, placed it on the rug, picked up a bear and gave that to her. And so they went until they had gone through all seven animals.

Satisfied, Henry sat down on his rug again.

"See what I mean?" Hart groused. He spooned perfectly-cooked scrambled eggs onto a plate, spread jam on the toast and cut it into bite-sized squares. "He's not about to choose just one."

"Hmm. A bachelor in the making?"

"Funny. And no. I imagine Henry will be like his dear old dad when he grows up and be a One Woman Man."

Another shimmer of awareness sifted through her.

Their eyes met.

Hart smiled and walked over to Henry. He knelt in front of him. "Henry, it's time for breakfast."

The toddler grabbed a stuffed animal and tucked it under his arm, but did not protest as Hart carried him back to the high chair and settled him in it. Once there, Hart traded a small plastic bowl of Cheerios for the animal, then went back to get the rest of Henry's breakfast.

"The problem is, I can't exactly take all seven of the animals with us wherever we go."

Maggie sat down at the table, too. This was where her expertise as a former nanny came in handy. She smiled reassuringly. "He'll settle on one. They always do. Although it may take a while."

Hart sighed. "I sure hope you're right about that." He brought a platter of scrambled eggs and bacon to the table which was already set for two adults and a child.

"This stuffed animal stage won't last forever…I promise." Maggie separated egg into bite-sized pieces for Henry. She put them on a plastic plate with a race car on it. He turned it upside down, dumping the egg onto his high chair tray, then handed the plate back to her.

Hart and Maggie grinned and simultaneously shook their heads. Just like parents. Only there was only one parent.... She was—actually, she wasn't exactly sure what she was to Henry except maybe a family friend.

"Well, at least he's consistent." Hart got up to make some more toast. "He likes to give as well as receive."

So does his daddy, Maggie thought, then immediately pushed the erotic memory away. She really needed to stop that.

"So did you have a particular lovey as a child?" Hart asked, bringing the conversation around to safer territory.

"I had a pink thermal blanket with a fancy braided trim that kept having to be replaced. But as far as toys, my favorite thing changed from year to year."

A few moments later, the toaster popped up. Hart tossed four slices on a plate and brought it to the table along with a tub of spreadable butter and several different kinds of jam.

"What about you?" Maggie asked, unable to help but admire his adeptness in the kitchen. "What were your favorite toys?"

He shrugged, looking momentarily baffled. "I don't know. I can't recall anything in particular. There's one way to find out, though." He disengaged his cell phone from the charger on the kitchen counter, and quickly texted. "My mom will know."

He'd barely had time to freshen their coffees and sit back down before his phone chimed. He read the screen and laughed. Then handed it to Maggie. In response to the question, "Did I have a lovey when I was a kid?" His mom had written, "Yes. You had me. And of course, your father."

They both laughed. Henry joined in.

When their chuckling had subsided, Maggie and Hart continued to eat their breakfast in companionable silence. Finally, she said, "Okay, so maybe as an only child you weren't all that into transitional objects. But it would be good for your son."

Hart wiped the jam from Henry's face. "I agree. And you know what else is good for Henry? You."

HART'S JOKING COMMENT reverberated in Maggie long after he'd darted upstairs to get a quick shower while she did dishes and watched over Henry, who was busy painting jam circles on his plastic high chair tray and finishing the last of his Cheerios.

She knew Hart had been sort of serious, referencing his son's need for her. She also knew, from offhand comments that his parents had made, that although Hart had rarely dated, he had been chased relentlessly by many of the local girls. They also indicated that except for his one failed engagement, he had never really been committed to anyone.

Not a really good track record, if that data were accurate.

Going strictly on business analysis methods, Hart Sanders was not a good bet for anything long term. Yet, even knowing that, she couldn't help but want more of the spectacular lovemaking they had shared the evening before.

And what, she wondered, did that say about her? And her own reliability?

"Out," Henry said, already trying to scramble out of his seat. "Me out."

Maggie smiled. "No problem, little guy. But first," she reached for the container of baby wipes on the counter, "we have to clean you up."

Henry frowned and began trying to release the catch of the seat belt around his waist. "Out."

Maggie tickled him slightly as she worked. "Wash up first."

He giggled. "Out!" he yelled playfully. "Mommy! Me! Out!"

Oooohhh. They really needed to do something about that. Especially since he had yet to call Hart Daddy.

"Maggie." She paused to point to her chest. "My name is Maggie. Your name is Henry." She indicated him.

Henry shook his head vehemently. "No," he said, giggling again. "Mommy!"

HART HEARD THE commotion in the kitchen. He rounded the corner to see Maggie stripping off Henry's jam-streaked knit shirt, undoing the restraint, then lifting the tyke out of the high chair. Unaware they had an audience, she danced Henry around and bussed the top of his little head. "You are so silly, you know that?"

Henry snuggled against Maggie's chest, looking completely besotted.

Hart knew exactly how his son felt.

He stepped over the gate and held up the clean shirt. "Thought you might need this."

"Would you look at that," Maggie said brightly. "*Daddy* brought you a clean shirt. Isn't that nice of *Daddy*?"

Henry merely smiled, hid his face in Maggie's shoulder and said "Mommy" yet again.

Touched by what Maggie was trying to do, Hart helped get the clean shirt on his son, then a pair of shoes. "He'll get there eventually. Just like with the loveys. In the meantime, isn't it about time for the Jaworskis?"

"And Pete Jacobson, the conductor for the Double Knot ranch steam train. He's agreed to drive the family to the top of the mountain for me." Maggie handed Henry over to Hart and waved at the husky gray-haired man at the back door.

Half a foot shorter than Hart, he strode in and promptly wrapped Hart—and Henry by default—in a big bear hug. "I heard you were back! And with a son, no less!"

Hart beamed, unable to hide his happiness and pride.

"Pete, meet Henry," Hart said. "Henry, Mr. Jacobson."

Pete bent down so they were at eye level and soberly shook Henry's hand. "Pleased to meet you, little man." Pete winked, then leaned closer and asked conspiratorially. "Why don't you see if you can get your daddy to stay this time?"

Hart winced. Back to that…again? "Did my mom pay you to say that?" he demanded.

Pete straightened and stuck his chest out importantly. "Didn't have to. I know how both your folks feel!"

Pete looked at Maggie. "Give me half an hour and I'll have the train at the loading station, ready to go."

Maggie smiled. "Thanks, Pete."

After the older gentleman left, Hart turned to Maggie. "Speaking of business…do you want the two of us to tag along today? Help you book the event?"

He flashed his most winning smile and looked deep into her eyes. She'd said she wanted to make love once. And they had. He wanted more, but did she? There was no telling from her calm, cheerful demeanor.

But that didn't mean he was giving up.

And one way to get back in her bed was to get closer in other ways. Perhaps return one of the many favors she'd done him in the last couple of days. He stepped close enough to let Henry work his magic, too. "My son's pretty darn charming, you know."

Maggie's face took on a maternal glow. She reached out to ruffle Henry's hair. "He is at that." She tilted her face up to Hart's. "I'd love the help."

Pleased, Hart promised, "Then we're on it."

Hart took Henry off to put a clean diaper on and find a cap. Maggie grabbed her jacket and went over to the office to greet the guests as they arrived. Forty minutes later, they had a group of thirty people ready to load the train.

Maggie took the microphone at the front of the rail car, while Hart settled in the conductor's jump seat, with Hart on his lap, and surveyed the crowd. Lynette Jaworski and her fiancé, Ben Bauer, still seemed lukewarm at best. Mr. and Mrs. Jaworski, however, were as enthusiastic as Hart's parents had indicated.

"I can't believe you're here, Hart. You were at our wedding," Mrs. Jaworski gushed, coming up to say a personal hello before taking her seat. "You had a cute little engineer's outfit and a cap. How adorable that you're back, helping out your folks, with your very own son."

"Temporarily," Maggie interjected. "Normally, Hart lives in California."

"But whenever I am here, I help out," Hart added nonchalantly.

Lynette Jaworski studied him, too. Finally, her fiancé frowned and said, "You look familiar."

Hart nodded. "You saw me the other day, at the office." For all of the two minutes you were there.

"No," Ben argued. "Like I've seen you before. Lots of times. Like in a movie or on TV or something."

Hart had no idea what they were talking about. But clearly, he noted, Maggie did.

She smiled at everyone like she was asking for trouble. "Do you read *Personalities!* magazine, or *Stars Weekly?*"

Nods—and a lot of interest—from quite a few people sitting in the car.

He had a sinking feeling in his gut that he was not going to like what came next.

Maggie gestured at him and said with a surprising amount of pride. "Hart is the head of Monica Day's security team. He's always there, somewhere close by or in the background, when his boss is out in public. So, he's in many of the photographs of Monica greeting her adoring fans."

Hart swung around to stare at Maggie, completely flummoxed. "I am?"

She looked at him like he was the silliest man on earth. "You didn't know that?"

He shrugged. "I don't read gossip magazines."

One of the bridesmaids was busy surfing the web with her smartphone. "Maggie's right!" she announced with a startled gasp. "Here's a picture of Hart at the Los Angeles premiere of Monica's Day new romantic comedy! He's right here!" She held it up for everyone to see.

And suddenly, thanks to Hart's exciting new "celebrity" status, the previously doubtful Lynette Jaworski was a lot more interested in having her wedding at the Double Knot Wedding Ranch.

Chapter Eight

Early that evening, Maggie paused in the doorway of Frank Sanders's workshop. Boxes of unassembled toys were stacked next to the work table. Hart was reading the directions in one hand and searching the toolbox with his other.

Maggie smiled and moved closer, taking in everything about him in one long surreptitious glance. For starters, he hadn't shaved at all that day, and stubble on his jaw gave him a pure male vibe that resonated deep within the most feminine parts of her. His sandy brown hair was mussed, and he'd exchanged the button-up he'd been wearing earlier in the day for a torso hugging army-green T-shirt that ended just south of his belt. Which left a lot of what was tucked inside his worn, snug jeans available for perusing.

Not that she needed to guess what was contained within said jeans. The memory of his incredibly hot physique was seared into her brain, fueling dreams that she'd promised herself would never be acted on again.

And that being the case, Maggie knew she had no choice but to pull herself together. She squared her shoulders, moved closer and held out a tall glass of icy lemonade.

"It looks like Christmas in here."

Hart put down the wrench and the instructions with a wink. Accepting the drink she handed him, he took a long, thirsty drink. "Got to make up for all the Christmases and birthdays I missed."

She leaned against the worktable and checked out the baby monitor plugged in nearby. "Put that way, spoiling him like crazy makes sense."

He smiled and met her eyes, sharing the mood as only someone could who'd spent the day co-operatively caring for, and chasing down, his tornado of a toddler son. "I also have an ulterior motive. A busy Henry is a happy Henry. And having stuff to do and explore keeps Henry very well occupied."

"Plus all this activity—" she gestured at the abundance of gifts "—helps him develop his brain. A very important thing for the young and growing."

Dimples appeared on either side of his lips. "I like the way you think."

And I like your soul-deep generosity. In bed, and out. In fact, I like damned near everything about you but the fact that you'll soon be leaving. Maggie inhaled. She'd come in here for an actual purpose—not just to gawk at him like a moon-eyed schoolgirl—she folded her arms in front of her. "So do you want the good news or the bad news?"

He set his glass down and went back to assembling wheels to the body of a toddler scooter. "Good first. Always."

"The Jaworski family is ready to sign a contract to have their wedding here. But only," she winced, revealing the catch, "if you will be part of the bride's security team."

Hart looked at her, brows raised. "Does she need a security team?"

"I think you're missing the point. She wants the cachet of having the head of Monica Day's security team at her wedding, watching over her."

Hart tested the wheels for sturdiness, front and back. "Ah."

"So, what do you think?"

Hart shrugged, apparently none too pleased to be used like that. "If it brings in business, I'll do it."

Cautiously, Maggie added the next condition. "And her parents want Henry to be there, if at all possible. In engineer garb for old time's sake." She reached into the pocket of her skirt.

"They also dug up this picture and emailed it to me a little while ago."

Hart leaned in so his broad chest bumped her shoulder. "Wow." He leaned in even closer, his warm breath brushing against her cheek. "I really was cute."

Maggie chuckled. "And modest, too."

Hart remained where he was, which was close enough to kiss her. "You seem happy," he noted affectionately.

Maggie was. She smiled up at him, wishing she hadn't vowed they'd make love only once. "This wedding is going to really help with the bottom line."

"Things are that tough?"

The concern in his voice prompted an onslaught of guilt. Leery of creating a problem, where there currently was none, Maggie turned away. "You and I should not be talking about this."

"You're right," Hart said in the hard-edged tone he always used when he thought she was running away. "I can just ask my folks. And they'll tell me. The conversation will then deteriorate into why I didn't join the family business the way I should have when I got out of the army, because if I had, the business wouldn't be in such dire straits."

Maggie came back to face him. "That's not really true."

"I know." Hart rooted around in the box for the plastic handgrips. "So, you're the business analyst." He worked them on either end of the silver handlebars. "Tell me what you would do to improve things if it were strictly up to you."

"Well, first of all, I'd hire someone to create a social media presence for The Wedding Train and the Double Knot Wedding Ranch. I'd try to get a video montage of a number of different weddings to post so people could look at the possibilities. I'd amp up the Old West aura of the steam train and the party barn, and maybe have an 1880s-style photographer available to create really unique wedding portraits in addition to the usual color photos." She took a breath. "And finally, I'd build a kitchen and bakery on the ranch, so we wouldn't have to rely on San Antonio caterers to provide the food."

"What about the lodging?"

"I'd leave that as is and continue to use San Antonio hotels for that."

Hart regarded her admiringly. "You've given this a lot of thought."

"I've been working here a long time. But, as you and I both know, it's not my place to make these decisions."

He fastened the seat on the scooter, then finished and set it aside. The very hint of a smile touched his mouth as he looked at her. "What if I told you it could be?"

Once again, he seemed to be two steps ahead of her. "What do you mean?"

"I've put a lot of money aside the last few years, so my parents could afford to retire when the time came. I'd be willing to invest part of that in the business, providing I get some say so. And that would include you staying on at least as long as it takes to make all the changes you outlined to me."

Not exactly what the romantic side of her wanted. The business side, either. "That's a lot of responsibility."

He remained confident. "I watched you today with the Jaworski-Bauer wedding party. You were amazing. But you're right—if you say yes to this, you would need an increase in salary. I'd make that happen, too."

It wasn't about money. It was about what would make her happy. Suddenly needing to sit down, Maggie opened up a camp chair propped against the wall and lowered herself into it. "Your parents will never go for this."

"They wouldn't have in the past." His gaze was level, serious. "But things are different now. We have Henry to consider. They're going to want to be a big part of his life, and that means turning over the day-to-day responsibilities for the wedding ranch to someone else. I'd like it to be you."

Maggie paused. "I'm flattered by your faith in me."

"But?"

"I'm not sure the impossibly long hours a move like that would require would jive with my plans to have a baby on my own."

"I'd provide money for you to hire extra staff so you could cut back on your own hours, plus whatever else you need. As long as you commit to heading up the operation."

Once again, Maggie thought, he was a man intent on getting what he wanted. And once again, despite her own reservations, she was tempted to give him exactly what he desired.

Oblivious to the conflicted nature of her thoughts he lifted a staying palm. "You don't have to give me an answer now. But I'm going to need to know your decision before I present this idea to them."

Glad for the reprieve, Maggie nodded in

agreement. "Okay…fair enough." The unexpected business meeting over, Maggie forced a sensible smile. She rose on shaking legs, refolded and replaced the chair, then headed back to the kitchen, silently chastising herself all the while.

She really had to get a grip.

What had she been expecting?

A proposal?

HART DIDN'T NEED an emotion detector to realize he'd upset Maggie. With the exception of her stint as a runaway bride, he'd never seen her make such a hasty retreat. The question was, did this mostly have to do with the fact she'd be missing Henry? Or was he involved somewhere here, too?

He knew he was sure as heck going to be missing her. The thought of even a day without her made his gut clench, and why that was, he had no idea.

It wasn't like they were anything special, or

ever going to be, given her irrevocable decision to keep him at arm's length. Then again, maybe this was a sign she wasn't as set in her decision as she pretended to be.

There was one way to find out.

Leaving the rest of the unassembled toys for another time, Hart picked up the finished scooter and carried it into the house. He was setting it down on the rug in the breakfast room, intending to go search for Maggie, when a crash in the pantry alerted him. He rushed through the semi-dark kitchen to find out the cause.

"Ouch!" Maggie muttered, hunched in a corner, rubbing her arm. At her feet had fallen a plastic container of flour. With the lid off, it was not so air-tight, however.

"What are you doing?"

Her blouse half-untucked, her slim skirt sliding up her world-class thighs, she put out a slender hand and worked to regain her balance. For the first time since they'd met, she looked completely immune to his charm.

"What does it look like I'm doing?" She brushed a sliding heap of flour off her lap, then stood, looking even more irritable. "Cleaning up."

His gaze tracked the softness of her lips and the flush in her cheeks. Somewhere between Henry's dinner and bath, she'd put her hair up again in a loose twist on the back of her head. Tendrils escaped, slanting provocatively across her forehead and the nape of her neck. Resisting the urge to haul her close and press a string of kisses up the slope of her throat, he said casually, "Before that."

She let out a quiet, defeated sigh. "I was going to make brownies, but that was before the mess."

Brownies sounded good. Especially if they were homemade. He rescued what was left inside the canister. "There's still enough here, I think. I'll even help."

I'll do anything I can to bring that smile back.

She tilted her head as if seeking to understand. "Why?" Her word was soft, plaintive. It echoed in the silence of the kitchen, broken only by the quiet buzz of the baby monitor.

Good question. Why was he flirting with her, when she'd already made it clear none of this could go anywhere except friendship and he wanted a lot more than that? A woman to come home to. A loving home and mother for his son...

Hart shrugged, still watching her sexy derriere. "Because I'm hungry." He was always hungry when he was around her. "Dinner was a long time ago." Lovemaking, even longer.

"Fine." She turned to set the oven dial to three-fifty.

"What should I do?"

"Nothing. I'm good."

She didn't look so good. She looked ticked off. At more than just the mess in the pantry. Still trying to figure out what was going through that beautiful head of hers, he refilled his glass of lemonade and pulled a stool up to the kitchen island.

In short order, eggs, baking powder, salt, cocoa, sugar and flour appeared on the counter. Butter was dropped into a bowl and put in the microwave to melt.

He realized he loved watching her cook.

She cracked two eggs with more than necessary force, then measured ingredients into a bowl. "You're really just going to sit there and watch me?"

"And keep you company," he said with a mischievous wink.

She bent over to get a baking pan out of the cupboard. Watching her, it took everything he had to stifle a groan.

Nonchalantly, he continued, "As it happens, I have a few questions of my own this evening."

She turned. To his frustration, looking more wary than ever. "Such as?"

"How long have you been following me in the gossip magazines?"

MAGGIE HAD KNOWN that question was coming; it had only been a matter of when. Ignoring his calm, steady stare, she said, "It was your mother who showed me the first photo of you at Monica Day's elbow, while she was working the rope line at some event. A friend of theirs had sent it to her."

That would not have been a big deal. The problem was, she had kept that emailed photo in a file on her computer and had added a whole lot more since. Why, she couldn't say, except that she had always been fascinated with Hart. Always wondered what made him so restless and ready to move on. Whereas all she wanted was a place where she could settle down and raise a family. Reading her mind, he smiled. "But you kept watching."

Maggie felt a rush of heat that had absolutely nothing to do with what she was doing over the stove. She poured melted butter into the other ingredients. "I like to keep up on current events."

He watched her carry the bowl over to the stand mixer and switch it on. "Mine?"

Maggie lounged against the counter, then blurted, "Your ego knows no bounds. You know that, don't you?"

He chuckled.

"But as long as we're on the subject of celebrity bosses," Maggie pushed on, deciding to use the opportunity to satisfy *her* curiosity, "how did you wind up working for Ms. Day?"

"I met Monica overseas, when she was on a USO tour for the troops. I was one of the guys who escorted her around. When she left, she gave me her card and asked me to let her know when it was time for me to re-enlist. She might have a better offer for me…"

And of course, Maggie thought, pouring batter into the pan and sliding it into the oven, Monica had.

"So when the time came, I called. She offered me a place on her security detail. When the head guy left to spend more time with his family, I took the top position."

"Pretty cool job." It was no wonder Hart didn't want to give it up.

His gaze stroked her features, each one, ending with her eyes. "I've sure seen a lot more of the world than I would have."

The delicious smell of baking chocolate began to fill the kitchen. "Is that why you joined the military?"

"There were two reasons. I wanted to go to Duke University in North Carolina. An ROTC scholarship was the only way I could afford to attend. I also wanted to do my part and serve my country."

She got out two spoons and slid onto the stool next to him. "Well, then, thank you for your service."

He mock saluted her. "You are most welcome, ma'am."

She handed him a spoon. Together, they

scraped the last of the rich chocolate batter from the bowl.

Another really bad idea.

Maggie looked at the baby monitor. "Henry sure is sleeping well tonight."

Hart nodded, relieved. "Between his antics last night and the train ride today, he was exhausted."

"Maybe he'll sleep through the night."

Hart dropped the spoon into the bowl and pushed it away. "That is my sincere hope. Which begs the question." He swiveled to face her. "What will you and I do in the meantime?"

Chapter Nine

Maggie knew all along that Hart would eventually make another move on her. But what she hadn't been able to figure out was what her response would be. Despite her previous declaration that they'd never make love again, she still wanted him. Maybe more than ever.

But given how hard and fast she was already falling for him, she should probably be careful. "Shouldn't you be planning to go to bed soon, too?"

Chuckling, he pulled her against him. "Oh, but I am."

Desire floated through her, whisper-soft. She

splayed her hands across the hardness of his shoulders and arched against him, unable to feel enough, get enough, and he hadn't even kissed her yet. "I meant for sleep."

His hands slid down her hips. "I plan on that, too." He caught her lower lip and drew it into his mouth, then laved it tenderly with his tongue. "Eventually."

Oh, dear heaven. She caught her breath, savoring everything about him, especially his ability to get his way. "This is…"

Smiling sexily, he went to work on the other side, kissing his way along the inside of her collar to the sweet spot just beneath her ear. "So right?"

She shuddered at the sensual feel of his lips on her skin and closed her eyes. He made her feel so alive. She jerked in an uneven breath, still struggling for control. "Way too complicated," she corrected.

And yet…

He pressed a light kiss to her temple then

drew back. "Listen to me, Maggie," he murmured. "If there's one thing I learned in the military, it's never to put off what you may never have another chance to do." He scored his thumb across her lower lip, continuing gruffly, "You've got to seize the moment in this life."

And seizing the moment meant making love with him.

Here. Now. With brownies baking in the oven and the baby upstairs fast asleep.

His hand dropped to the buttons on her blouse. Undoing one, then another. Sliding his palm inside. She shuddered in anticipation. He kissed her again, deeply, evocatively, until she was arching against him, tingling all over.

He broke off the kiss, looked deep into her eyes. "You know what I want at this moment?"

She shifted her hips, encountering rock solid hardness, searing heat. She had an idea, even as she wrapped her arms around his neck. "The same thing I want," she whispered. "For you to be my much-needed rebound guy, at least as long as you're here."

Finally, something to hit the Pause switch, even though it wasn't quite what she intended. Hart drew back, not as appreciative of her resolutely practical attitude as she would have hoped.

"Wow." He looked like she had sucker punched him. "Already running away before we've even hooked up again." He shook his head in silent admonition. "I think that's a record, Maggie, even for you."

"There you go with the jokes again."

He mimed an arrow to the center of his chest. "Got to do something to dull the pain."

Hands on his shoulders, she brought his comically staggering form upright. "Listen to me, Hart," she said seriously. "We have to be realistic."

He shifted her so she was sitting on the counter. Her skirt hiked up to mid-thigh, and he slid his palms beneath the hem. "Why do you figure that?"

She quivered as his caressing palm went even higher. She clamped her hands over his to still their progress. "Because now you have Henry to consider, and that means you need someone for the long term." *Someone who could commit to a lifetime.* "Someone you'd want to settle down with and marry. Not someone to play house with."

He challenged her with a look. "And you're only a short term kind of gal, is that it?" The way he said it made her feel he didn't believe it any more than she wanted it to be so. But it was the God's honest truth.

"I'm saying I'm not the kind of woman you should love…but lust is apparently a very different matter."

Because the lust he was evoking was driving her crazy with longing, even though he still hadn't resumed kissing her!

He wrapped his arms about her waist and

shifted her all the way to the edge of the counter. Eyes smoldering, he lifted her legs, wrapped them around his waist. Exhaling, he angled his face very close to hers. "Stop talking, Maggie. Stop putting up roadblocks to happiness. And most of all, stop pushing me away, and just let us be, let yourself feel…"

And then he did kiss her again. He kissed her until she lost all track of what they had been saying and what she meant to say. Until she lost sight of all the reasons why they shouldn't be doing this.

He kissed her until she moaned and surged into his touch and her panties hit the floor. His jeans followed.

His possession of her was fast, fierce and completely raw. There was nothing of the rebound about it. When it ended, she was shaken to the core. And this time, she did not pull away.

MAGGIE WOKE HOURS LATER, alone in her own bed. But the warmth of the sheets beside her told her Hart hadn't been gone for long. The wild giggling on the baby monitor on her nightstand said both he and his son had awakened in a delightful mood.

Body tingling from the repeated lovemaking they had enjoyed during the night, she pushed herself up on her elbows in time to see Hart walk into the room, a fully dressed Henry in his arms.

"Mommy!" Henry yelled, holding out his arms for her.

When Hart set the toddler down on the mattress, Henry toddled over to her and launched himself into her arms. Sighing contentedly, he placed his head on her chest, looked up at her and flashed a great big smile. "Hi," he said.

"Hi, Henry," Maggie replied softly, smiling back.

Henry demanded, "Toys."

Hart ruffled his son's hair. "I'll get them."

He returned with all seven stuffed animals and the blanket. He set them all on the bed and dropped down beside them as Henry engaged in another game of pretend play. Hart stretched out on his side, head propped on his upraised hand. The grin he gave her was all sexual mischief. "So, how'd you sleep?"

Maggie blushed. "I think you know the answer to that."

The glimmer in his eyes said he sure did.

And so their morning began with the three of them hanging out like any other happy family. Except they weren't a family, Maggie reminded herself, as the sweet sentimental time went on.

And at the rate they were going—with Hart making love to her one moment, and the next, urging her to stay behind and oversee the ranch while he resumed his life in California—they never would be.

"YOU SOUND DOWN," Callie said, when Maggie called her later in the morning, just to say hello. Hart had taken Henry into town to purchase a baby swing and a sandbox for outdoor play. Maggie had stayed behind to get caught up on the RSVPs for the upcoming Randolph-Albertson wedding.

"I'm fine." Maggie stacked the salmon entrée responses in one pile, the steak in another.

"Hart?"

Maggie opened another envelope. "How did you guess?"

"Easy. I've seen the man. He is one hot cowboy."

"Too hot," Maggie muttered, recalling all over again how unrestrained their lovemaking had been.

"Did he make a pass at you?"

Maggie wasn't sure how to answer that. So she didn't.

"Need a chaperone until his parents get back from Australia?"

Maggie didn't know how to answer that, either.

Callie sighed and chided, "You know, you really should stop running from everything fun."

"I'm not running." But deep down, she knew she kind of was. She had started the day of her wedding-that-wasn't, and had never stopped.

"Everything doesn't have to be forever," her twin said. "Because even when we want it to be, it isn't always long term."

Abruptly, Maggie was reminded she wasn't the only Jackson and Lacey McCabe daughter who had suffered the slings and arrows of love. Chastened, she inquired gently, "Are we talking about your marriage?"

"Brief as it was. My point is, I didn't appreciate what I had when I should have. I was always waiting for what was around the bend. Thinking if only this or that happened then Seth and I would finally be content. And I would have been, Maggie, if I'd just been able to live in the moment."

Score one for Hart, Maggie thought.

He now had the ever-practical, way too romantic Callie on his side.

"IS THAT EVEN?" Hart asked, two hours later.

Happy to be back in the presence of her handsome "rebound guy" and his charming son, Maggie surveyed the molded plastic baby swing Hart had attached from the lowest branch of a sturdy oak tree. A thick rubber pad beneath the sturdy metal chain protected the bark from being eroded and kept the chain from sliding down the branch.

"I think so," she said. She scooped up the roaming toddler and situated him comfortably in her arms. "We won't really know until we put Henry in the seat and see if he's at a slant."

Hart studied the situation with a skeptical eye. "That's what I was hoping to avoid."

Noting he had shaved again—to prevent the razor burn he had given her the night before—Maggie pivoted to face him and felt desire waft through her all over again. "You could count the links."

Hart ran a hand across his jaw. "Except the branch isn't exactly straight to begin with."

"True," Maggie concurred.

"Henry, this is going to be trial and error," Hart said.

Henry looked up at Hart. "Har…" he said, clear as day.

Maggie and Hart looked at each other in stunned amazement. "Did he just try and say your name?" Maggie asked thickly.

"Har," Henry repeated again, staring adoringly up at Hart.

Joy lit Hart's face, and Maggie put her hand over his chest. "This is *Daddy*, Henry. *Daddy*. I'm Maggie." She pointed to herself. Then to him. "You're *Henry*."

Henry smiled at Maggie. "Mommy," Henry said, even more clearly and precisely.

Maggie ducked her head in defeat.

Hart laughed ruefully.

Maggie was glad he had a sense of humor but also knew it wouldn't be funny for long. It had to hurt that Henry refused to acknowledge him as his daddy. She sent Hart a sympathetic look and received one of gratitude in return. "We'll keep working on it," she promised, as a car headed up the lane toward the ranch house.

Hart squinted. "Do you have any appointments this afternoon?"

Maggie shook her head.

The car stopped. An attractive young woman with a platinum blond bob got out. She was dressed nicely and looked to be in her early-to mid-twenties. Hand shading her eyes, her movements purposeful, she strode toward them. "I'm looking for Maggie McCabe."

Hoping they were about to get another new client, Maggie smiled brightly. "You found her."

Abruptly, some of the light went out of the young woman's expression. "I'm Gus's girlfriend, Nancy Lindholm. Can we talk?"

FOR A MOMENT, a staggeringly uncomfortable silence fell. Hart casually introduced himself and his son to their visitor, then turned and looked at Maggie. "You got this?"

Maggie knew what Hart really meant was: *Are you okay with this? Because if not, I'm here for you.*

Appreciating his protectiveness, even if she didn't need it, she nodded. "We'll be over in the office." This was after all, her problem. Not his.

Maggie led the way across the breezeway and into the building. On the way to her office, she stopped in the break room and grabbed two bottles of chilled peach tea. She handed one to Nancy and settled behind her desk. Nancy took an armchair on the other side.

She glanced curiously at the adjacent play area, which was messy with Henry's toys, then turned back to Maggie. A few pleasant-ries passed then Nancy finally got to the point. "I need to know what happened to make you run out on Gus in the middle of the wedding ceremony."

Remembering her promise to Gus to do her best to allay Nancy's anxieties, Maggie stalled. "What has Gus told you?"

"That you ran off in the woods. Hart chased you. Gus followed. He was unable to talk you into marrying him, so he went back to call off the wedding. And you made your way back to the ranch with Hart. Is that correct?"

"Yes." Those were the facts.

"So what was going on? Were you having an affair with Hart Sanders while you were engaged to Gus? Because I have to say, the two of you looked pretty cozy now."

They were cozy, Maggie thought. More so with every moment that passed. But that was none of Nancy's business. Or anyone else's for that matter. Maggie shook her head. "I didn't even know Hart then. He just followed me to keep me, and others in our wedding party who might have given chase, too, from getting lost."

Nancy sighed and looked even more confused. She rubbed her temple as if feeling a giant headache coming on. "Then what is Gus keeping from me? Because I know there's something he's not telling me."

Maggie had no idea whether Gus still felt as smothered by family as he had then. She could also understand why Gus wouldn't want to admit to everything he'd said to her after the rehearsal dinner. His suggestion that they ditch their families and move as far away as possible put him in a bad light. And worse, would make Nancy, if she cared about her loved ones even half as much as Maggie cared about hers, more nervous and uncertain. "What happened was a long time ago." A lifetime ago, in fact. For all she knew, Gus felt differently now. The point was, she hadn't asked. And without clarification…

"I still need to know."

Maggie suddenly had an idea how Hart must feel when he was around her and her doubts. "Why?"

Nancy frowned. "Because I'm not going to

say yes to a guy who keeps secrets from me! And finding out he'd been with someone for seven whole years, a woman he'd actually lived with, and then had that person run out on him on their wedding day, is a pretty big red flag, if you ask me."

Maggie couldn't argue that point. Gus was going to have to be a lot more open and honest if he ever wanted to have an enduring relationship. But that was between him and Nancy.

So Maggie went back to what she could openly discuss without violating her and Gus's agreement to keep everything between them private. She lifted a hand. "Look, Gus did not want to call off our wedding. That was all on me—because I didn't tell him about the doubts I was feeling earlier. So you *can't* blame him for that."

"There's more to it than what either of you have said." Nancy studied Maggie, her feminine intuition evidently working full force.

"There's a reason why he had to talk to you first before I could see you."

Nancy was right about that. But Maggie did not know how to address it while maintaining her own integrity. Like it or not, any further details really had to come from Gus.

Nancy's head lifted. Abruptly, she went so still, Maggie knew there was someone behind her. Her spirits sinking and pulse jumping, Maggie swiveled, half expecting to see Gus standing there in the doorway. It was Hart.

With Henry clasped in his arms, he looked tough and sexy in his usual indomitable way. Relief poured through her, followed swiftly by yet another wave of anxiety.

When, Maggie wondered, would she ever really be able to put the past, and the mess she had made of it, behind her?

Ignoring the escalating tension in the office, Hart strolled on in with Henry babbling all the while. "Hey," Hart said with a smile, acting as if he hadn't just heard what Nancy'd said, when Maggie could tell that he clearly had. Handsome brow furrowed, he turned to Maggie. "Do you know if we have any more diapers? The ones that were in Henry's suitcase and diaper bag are all gone."

"I put the new package in the linen closet upstairs."

"Thanks." Hart gave Maggie a long look, making sure she was all right. Henry waved bye-bye and Hart disappeared again.

Maggie talked to Nancy a few more minutes, basically going over the same ground. Finally, they said goodbye.

Knowing she'd done nothing to allay Nancy's fears and instead had made them worse with her careful verbal dance, Maggie went upstairs. Hart was in the midst of changing a pretty stinky diaper, but he handled it like a champ. "What happened down there?" His look was protective.

Maggie sighed. "I was as honest as I could be without betraying Gus's confidence, or cause further hurt or humiliation for everyone involved." Because if either of their families knew how Gus had felt, they would have been devastated—they likely still would.

Hart wrapped the dirty diaper in a disposable plastic bag and dropped it in the airtight deodorizing diaper pail. Leaving Henry in the crib, he went to wash his hands in the adjacent bath. "So in other words, you lied by omission for the sake of your ex."

Maggie grabbed some air freshener and sprayed it in the hallway. "I wouldn't put it like that."

He gave her a telling look but made no response.

A few moments later, Hart lifted Henry out of the crib and they walked together down the stairs. "So, how did covering for him go?" Hart's tone was casual, but she sensed an underlying disapproval. As if he had expected better of her.

Irritated because she had done the best she

could under very difficult circumstances, Maggie lingered in the hallway, next to the stairs, one hand on the newel. "Nancy still doesn't trust Gus. It's almost as if now that she knows I ran away on our wedding day, Gus is damaged goods. At least in her view."

Hart set Henry down to run around. The little boy promptly leaned back against the front door, raced forward to the end of the hall, turned and raced back again.

Hart shrugged his broad shoulders. "Only the two of them can fix that."

Maggie flushed self-consciously. Beside them, an energetic Henry repeated the same action all over again.

"You're saying I shouldn't feel guilty for behaving the way I did that day?"

His gaze caressed her face. "Do you still feel guilty?"

It was an honest question. One that deserved a forthright answer. "I guess I do, a little." Even though she knew in her heart she had done what was best for everyone. Maggie swallowed around the sudden ache in her throat. "It's like there's a stigma attached to me because of the embarrassment I caused that I'm never going to get rid of no matter what I do."

In that respect, she and Gus were in the same boat.

Hart was silent a long moment, his expression inscrutable. "Only you can fix that."

"Thanks a heap," Maggie said tightly.

"Hey." He palmed his chest. "I call 'em like I see 'em. But I have faith you'll figure it all out."

The heat within her intensified, only now it was a different kind of heat and tension. The kind that usually preceded their lovemaking. "Thanks even more."

He grinned at her wry tone. "In the meantime, if you're not too busy, my son and I would like the pleasure of your company."

"Sure," Maggie said softly, tucking her hand in Hart's. She smiled as their glances meshed.

Said even more hopefully, "Why not?" She needed the peace and serenity only the Sanders "men" brought.

WITH HENRY FRESHLY diapered and Maggie on hand to help out with Henry for a little while, Hart went back out to set up the turtle-shaped sandbox. He put it in the shade, then poured in fifty pounds of white sand while Maggie opened up the bag of sandbox toys.

Short minutes later, she was sitting in the grass with Hart and his son enjoying a beautiful, sunny Texas afternoon.

The three of them might have stayed like that forever, playing at being a real family again, had a FedEx truck not come up the drive.

Hart turned to Maggie. "I think that's for me. Work."

Of course it was, Maggie thought. Despite the fact Hart was technically on emergency family leave from his job, demands had been coming from California nonstop since the moment he and Henry arrived. Email, phone, express delivery—there was always something needing his immediate attention.

Maggie watched as several packages came off the truck. Hart scribbled his name, chatted a moment longer with the delivery guy, then returned to her. "A couple things need my attention immediately. Do you mind?"

Maggie shook her head. Time to be pragmatic about this part of their lives, too. "No. Go right ahead. I'll look after Henry."

Despite Hart's absence, the next hour passed blissfully. The summer afternoon was unusually temperate, with the temperatures in the low eighties, the air dry. Eventually, they went inside and returned with Popsicles, which they ate in the grass, a distance away from the sandbox.

When Henry was finished, Maggie let him wash his hands off with the hose, a fact that resulted in a giggling fit and both of them getting a little wet.

Hart came out. He stood, hands on his hips. "Who's having fun without me?"

"Har…" Henry said enthusiastically.

Hart lifted his son in the air. "That's Daddy Har to you, buddy."

Henry giggled.

Happy to have him with them again, Maggie smiled, too.

They went back to the sandbox, spent another lazy hour sifting sand and pouring it through the funnel in a plastic cement-mixer-style sand toy. Until Henry frowned and tugged at his diaper irritably. "Off," he said, squirming. Then more impatiently, "Off!"

Hart looked at Maggie. "Think he's wet?"

"Maybe. Or he could have gotten a little sand in his diaper. He has been messing around in it for a while now."

"Well, let's go change you." Hart swept his son up in his arms.

Figuring they'd spent enough time outside, Maggie gathered the toys. She was just putting the lid back on the sandbox when Hart opened a window from the second floor. "Maggie," he shouted through the screen. "Come quick!"

Chapter Ten

The alarm in Hart's voice had her racing into the house and up the stairs. Hart was in the nursery, standing over the crib. Henry was standing up, sans diaper, banging both hands on the rail. From just above his waist to the top of his thighs he was covered with little red bumps that had not been there three hours before. No wonder little Henry had been complaining!

"Is this a diaper rash?" Hart asked.

Maggie referenced what she recalled from her babysitting years. "Not like any I've ever seen. I mean, usually a diaper rash comes on pretty slowly. You'll see a little bit of redness and irritation, but this…." She turned, unable to hide her worry. "I don't know, Hart."

For the first time since she'd known him, Hart looked scared. "Do you think he's getting sick?"

Maggie touched Henry's skin. It felt cool to the touch where there was a rash and where there was not. "He doesn't seem to have any fever. He's not crying."

Hart shoved a hand through his hair. "I probably should have gotten a pediatrician before now."

Speaking of which…Maggie lifted a hand. "My parents are at a medical conference in San Antonio this week." Which was just a forty-five minute drive away. "My mom is a pediatrician. I'll call her and see if I can catch her between lectures. She'll be able to advise us."

As it happened, Lacey Buchanon-McCabe did more than that. She offered to make a house call. Hart agreed. And an hour later, Maggie's parents were there.

"THANKS FOR COMING," Hart welcomed her parents warmly and was greeted kindly in return. This was a relief to Maggie. Both her parents could be tough critics when it came to their daughters' male friends. But at the moment, all attention was on the medical calamity at hand. Clad in a western sport-coat, open collared shirt, boots and jeans, her six-foot-plus dad looked as handsome and distinguished as ever. Her mom was equally well put-together in a sleek coral pantsuit with a sleeveless tunic style top.

Her short, honey-blond hair glinted in the evening sunshine as Lacey carried her medical bag inside. "Where's our little patient?" she asked with a smile.

Maggie led her parents to the living room, where Henry was sitting on the floor, playing with a couple of trucks. He had a diaper on, but no shorts. "You can see the rash is still spreading down his thighs, and above his waist," Maggie said.

It did not take Lacey long to diagnose. "It's an allergic reaction. Some sort of contact allergy. So what's new? Are you using any new creams in the diaper area? A different kind of baby wipe? A different kind of diaper?"

Maggie looked at Hart, suddenly realizing what it could be. "The new diapers we got from the store?"

"We just opened a bag."

Maggie went to get it. Her mom looked at the label. "These have aloe in them. I bet he's allergic to that."

"No one told us."

"They might not have known. Has this happened before?" she asked Hart.

"I don't know," he said. "I can check with his foster mother."

Jackson McCabe's brow lifted. "Henry was in foster care?"

Maggie ignored the sudden clenching in her abdomen. She pulled in a breath and attempted to quell the sudden anxiety rising within her. "Hart just found out he was a dad a week ago. He's doing his best to get up to speed."

"You don't have to defend me, Maggie," Hart said quietly. He looked at her father, then her mom, regret in his eyes. "I'm aware I screwed up. Otherwise I would have known about Henry long before now." His expression hardened. "It's not something I intend to have happen again."

Maggie hesitated a second too long. "Back to what we need to do for Henry..."

Lacey looked at Hart. "Did you get any medical records from foster care? Usually, they send some along."

Hart nodded and went to his laptop bag and pulled out an envelope provided by Sante Fe Department of Children and Family Services.

Lacey flipped through it. "Okay. He's current on all his shots and has no drug allergies that we know of, so it's safe to give him liquid Benadryl." She took a premeasured doser out of her bag, made a funny face at Henry to distract him and slid the syringe-style applicator between his lips. Henry swallowed it before he quite knew what was happening.

After Lacey threw the dispenser away, she turned toward Hart. "Do you have any other brand of diapers?"

Hart nodded. "The nighttime ones."

"I'll get them." Maggie went back up the stairs and brought down that package.

Her mom checked the label. "Good. No aloe. You can use these until you have a chance to get some more. In the meantime, we should probably get this little one in a baking soda bath." She patted Henry on the shoulder, and Henry reached out his arms to her. Before Lacey knew it, she had an armful of adorable baby boy.

More grandmother-to-be than physician now,

Lacey sighed wistfully. "Oh, I miss these days," she said, softly.

Maggie knew she was going to miss these days when Henry left, too. Ignoring the sudden press of tears behind her eyes and the even fiercer longing for a child of her own, she busied herself, finding the baking soda.

Visibly relaxed now that the emergency had been abated, Hart turned to her parents. "Would you like to stay for dinner?" He flashed an engaging smile. "Seems the least we can do, since you drove all the way out here to lend a hand, is throw a few steaks on the grill."

"We'd love to," Lacey said. While her dad seemed to reserve judgment once again.

"SO WHAT'S GOING ON?" Lacey asked Maggie, while the two of them watched over Henry in the bath. "And don't tell me nothing because I already know something's brewing by the way Callie clammed up the other day when I asked her if she had heard from you recently."

"Just because my twin sister likes to talk and for some reason didn't that day…"

"Mmm-hmm. I don't need to be a doctor to see into your mind, Magnolia McCabe. And neither does your father. How long has Hart been hanging around the Double Knot ranch?"

Maggie reached into the cupboard for a clean towel. "Since late last week."

Lacey sipped the apricot-flavored tea Maggie had provided. "And his parents are where?"

"On a cruise to New Zealand and Australia."

"Which leaves the two of you alone here."

Maggie propped her hands on her hips. "What are you trying to insinuate, Mom?"

"You and Hart are attracted to each other."

Maggie pushed aside the memory of their hot and frenzied lovemaking. "I'm attracted to a lot of people," she shot back. Aware how ridiculous that sounded, she flushed. "Mom, one step at a time. The only reason I haven't dated thus far is that there's no one to get serious about. This ranch is out in the middle of nowhere, literally and figuratively speaking!"

Her mother gave her a look that spoke volumes. "Which is exactly why you like being here so much, I'm guessing, even when Hart and Henry aren't around."

Maggie sighed. "You're beginning to sound like Callie."

Her expression tender, Lacey set her tea aside and knelt down to play with Henry, too. "And everyone else who cares about you and wants you to move on?"

Maggie's throat ached. She rose and rummaged through the cupboard for more of the new bath toys.

"I'm trying, Mom." Taking a little walk on the wild side with Hart had been the first step toward resuming a more normal life. She hadn't just stuck a toe in the water, she'd taken a cannonball off the high dive.

Once Hart left—and he was leaving in a mat-

ter of days—she would move on to more rea-
sonable, rational endeavors.

Like finding a way to really and truly move
on that didn't include falling in love with handsome ex-soldiers and babies that weren't really
hers.

As if realizing she was thinking about him,
Henry turned to Maggie. Maggie's heart
swelled with love as he reached down into the
water and fished out the only toy he'd brought
with him from foster care, his beloved bathtub
key-ring. "Mommy," he said, pressing it affectionately into her fingers. "Here. *Mommy.*"

A silence fraught with worry fell. Lacey
looked at Maggie and said softly, "Oh, honey,
be careful. Before you find yourself getting in
way too deep."

The ache in Maggie's throat grew. She felt
tears gathering behind her eyes. Stubbornly
refused to let them fall. "Meaning?"

Lacey wrapped a soothing arm around Maggie's shoulders. "Hart and Henry need you now. I see that. I'm glad you're here for them." She paused to let her words sink in. "Just bear in mind that crisis-born relationships fade in intensity once the crisis is over. Especially in situations with children."

And who would know better than her mother, a vaunted pediatrician with nearly thirty years of experience? "Or in other words, Hart wouldn't mean to hurt me," Maggie guessed, taking her mother's advice to heart. "Any more than Gus and I meant to hurt each other."

Lacey nodded, the concern in her kind eyes deepening. "But he might."

FOR THE SAKE of their company, Maggie did her best to present a cheerful facade for the rest of the evening. Still, it was a huge relief when her parents finally said goodnight and went back to the San Antonio hotel where the medical conference was being held.

"So, what did you and my dad talk about?" Maggie asked as they cleared the last of the coffee cups.

With Henry down for the night, the downstairs was quiet, the setting perfect for lovemaking.

"He's worried about you. He and your mom feel like they're partially to blame for you running out on Gus. He knows they pushed you to get married."

Maggie sighed. "Only because they believe very firmly that for a relationship to last, there must be commitment of the lifelong variety." *Unlike what we have, which is a very short-term arrangement, born out of sheer necessity and happenstance.*

"He knows they can't go back and change any of that."

"I sense a caveat in here somewhere."

"But he does think he and your mom can do more to protect you in the future."

Maggie groaned. "Which means what, exactly?"

"They want you to leave the ranch, and everything that happened here, behind. Move on with your life."

Which was nothing she hadn't heard before. Maggie studied him. "Did he ask you to help with that task?"

A telltale pause. Finally, Hart shrugged. "He thought you might listen to me."

Tension clenched her gut. "Did he say anything else?"

Hart regarded her carefully. "He's worried you might be getting too involved with Henry and me. He said leaving the babies you'd cared for had been difficult for you in the past."

No joke. "Yeah, it was hard. I'd get really close to these little kids over the course of a summer, and then I'd have to leave to go back to college. Often, by the time the next summer rolled around, the families had made other arrangements for their kids, and I'd have to start over with a whole new family. Of course, I'd end up getting close to them, too."

Too close, it had often seemed. Because leaving had always been hard.

Hart rested a gentle hand on her shoulder. "Do you ever hear from any of them?"

"Not really. It's usually better that way." Maggie had to turn away from the sympathy in his eyes. "The kids get adjusted to their new circumstances. And of course they have their families. Putting a former nanny in the center of all that just makes it harder on everyone."

He brought her all the way into his arms, the hardness and warmth of his body as soothing as his voice. "I'd want you to stay in touch with Henry."

"I know." Maggie rested her head against his chest, despite herself.

"But?" Hart asked.

Knowing she needed some time to sort things out alone, Maggie extricated herself from his embrace. "Maybe my parents are right." She headed for the stairs, more than ready to say good-night. "Maybe all this is getting a little too complicated."

To MAGGIE'S RELIEF, Henry proved an effective chaperone for the next couple of days. When he wasn't demanding their full attention, individual work demands kept both adults busy during what Maggie had privately dubbed the casual and cautious stage of her relationship with Hart.

Oblivious to the difficulty she was having implementing her decision to slow things down, Hart walked into the party barn, Henry in his arms. "They're baaaack!" he announced with all the gusto of a late night comedy show.

"I'm guessing you're not talking about your parents." Although Frank and Fiona Sanders were due to return by the end of the week.

Hart anchored an arm about her waist and pulled her close. "Nope."

She could feel the heat of his body and see the desire in his eyes. Her breath hitched in her chest. "Then who?"

"Your ex and his fiancée."

Gus and Nancy? Maggie blinked. "Why?"

"They want to speak with you, so I had them wait in the living room."

Maggie grinned, as Henry leaned over and bussed the top of Maggie's head, the way he'd seen Hart do. She shook her head and kissed Henry back. "I really wish they'd call first."

Henry giggled and kissed Hart's chin.

Hart returned the gesture and ruffled his son's hair, his eyes holding Maggie's all the while. "They're probably afraid you would tell them you were too busy to see them if they did." Which Maggie absolutely would have been tempted to do.

"Besides," Hart continued, "looks like a spur of the moment jaunt down here to me."

Maggie swore inwardly. Multiple times.

The grooves on either side of his lips deepened. "Want company? You can use me as a shield to make sure things don't get out of hand."

She stepped back far enough to be able to survey him head to toe. He was handsome no matter what he wore. Even if it was snug-fitting cowboy jeans and a worn chambray shirt with applesauce smeared across one sleeve. "Maybe I should request you for my own personal bodyguard," she teased.

He grinned in a way that kicked her heart rate up a notch. "You couldn't afford me."

So true, Maggie thought on a wistful sigh.

"Unless," mischief glimmered in his playful look, "you paid me with something other than cash."

Maggie stepped back, propped her hands on her hips, and tried not to objectify him any more than usual. "No wonder you have a rep as a heartthrob."

"Now, now." He winked. "Don't believe ev-

erything my not-so-objective mother has to say
on that subject."

Maggie didn't have to. She could see it for
herself. Hart Sanders was a thrill a minute, and
as her racing pulse indicated, always would be.
She was the one who needed to keep her defenses up. Unfortunately, it was getting harder
and harder for her to do so.

As MAGGIE EXPECTED, Gus appeared unhappy
and tense. Nancy was on a mission, and a not
very pleasant one at that. Deciding it would be
best to get this over with as quickly as possible,
Maggie sat down in an armchair opposite them
while Hart settled Henry down on the floor to
play with his stuffed animals. "What can I do
for you?" she asked.

"I want to see the locale where your ceremony was held," Nancy said.

Noting Gus looked even more miserable,
Maggie asked, "Why?" In cases like this, re-
enactments were never a good idea.

Nancy shrugged. "Because I'm thinking maybe Gus and I should have our wedding there."

Now Maggie really had to ask. "Why on earth would you want to do that?"

Nancy regarded her steadily. "To replace bad memories with good ones."

"I think for Gus that might taint an otherwise very happy situation," Maggie warned.

Hart shot a look at Gus, then said, "I think Gus can speak for himself, Maggie."

"As it happens…" Nancy folded her arms in front of her. "Gus already said no. He's only here to humor me and help me see what a bad idea it is."

"I have a feeling you're worried about more than just where to hold the wedding," Maggie said gently. They both knew, even if the men didn't, that Nancy had an ulterior motive for being here. "Why don't you tell me what this is really about?"

As always, understanding—and the opportunity to vent without judgment—went a long way toward solving the problem.

Nancy looked at Maggie a long moment, then finally admitted, still looking simultaneously upset and relieved, "I wanted to see the two of you together to see if there were any sparks. Obviously," Nancy said, even more quietly, "there are none."

At least they were all on the same page about that, Maggie thought with relief.

"But that doesn't explain why neither of you have told me the truth," Nancy continued.

And Maggie had to admit, Nancy had them there. In her place, she would be furious and upset, too.

Gus gave Maggie a look, practically begging her to stay silent.

Hart looked at Maggie, seeming to advise the opposite.

Knowing it would never be over unless Nancy did have the whole truth, and nothing but the truth, Maggie decided, "You're right. "

Her mind made up, Maggie turned to Gus and said bluntly, "This isn't going to work. Nancy will never trust you unless you tell her the whole story. So you've got to stop stonewalling her and trust that if you open your heart to her, she will understand." *The way Hart understands me.*

Gus set his jaw. "The past is over. It needs to stay over."

Maggie only wished that were possible. She'd learned the hard way that keeping her troubles buried deep inside where they could only fester was the wrong path to take. "Okay, then I will." Briefly, she turned to Nancy and explained everything that had happened the night after the rehearsal dinner, prompting her to search her soul and run away.

Nancy listened in silence, taking it all in. Finally, she turned to Gus. "Do you still feel that way about family?"

He shrugged. "Sometimes the demands of

both sets of parents and all our siblings get to be too much. But I think I'm a lot more willing to work it out now."

"Are you going to spring something crazy on me the night before our wedding, or ask me to move far away from everything and everyone we know? Because I have to tell you, I'm not willing to do that if we have kids, the way we've planned. In fact, I'm not willing to do that, period."

Gus took her hands in his and gazed into her eyes. "No. I love you."

Nancy evidently tried to trust in the sincerity of Gus's words. Finally, she looked at Maggie, still thinking, trying to decide.

Maggie stood. "The only reason Nancy is doubting you, Gus, is that none of this has come from you directly. You can change all that, if you'll just talk to her and tell her what's in your heart, from this point forward."

A silence fraught with heartache and uncertainty fell.

Seemingly aware there was nothing left to say, Nancy and Gus left, more dejected than ever.

Hart took Maggie in his arms. "They'll either work it out or they won't. For the record," he said, kissing her gently, "you did the right thing. The two of them needed the truth to be out there."

Maggie sighed. She'd done what she could to clear the air and make things right. Yet she was still aware it might not have been enough.

"Walk?" Henry came up to join them, clueless as to what had just been going on. He clasped their hands, then tugged them toward the front door. Once again, Maggie thought, they were a family, albeit a temporary one.

Hart looked at her. "What do you say? A little fresh air?"

Maggie nodded. She really needed the break the temperate sunny day would provide. "Sounds good to me. I'll get the sunscreen."

"And I'll get the stroller."

When they returned to the ranch house, a long relaxing time later, several more FedEx packages sat on the doorstep, a couple of them pretty big ones. Return address? Maggie didn't even have to look to know. Beverly Hills, California.

"THANKS FOR PUTTING Henry to sleep tonight," Hart said, several hours later.

"Glad to help. I know you were swamped with whatever arrived."

Although, Maggie noted pensively, Hart had only actually emptied two of the boxes. The third was open, with the bubble wrap still lying crookedly across the top, which meant whatever was in there was still inside. Not that it was any of her business.

Still, she had to wonder, why that one had been left untouched. It was always the loneliest in the evenings when Henry was asleep and her work was done. She ambled in restlessly.

"Anything I can do to help?" she asked. "Brew you a pot of coffee?"

He made a note on the page in front of him. "Already made some. There's more in the kitchen. Help yourself."

"Get you a brownie?"

He turned and gave her the lazy once-over. "Already had two."

The mischief in his gaze had her comically overreacting, too. "What?"

He laughed out loud, the sound as sexy as it was infectious. "I might have eaten the last one."

"That's okay." She patted her sides, ignoring the pleasure sifting through her. "My hips will thank you later."

He shook his head. "Nothing wrong with your hips."

Good to know. Maggie sauntered closer as a palpable silence fell. "So, what is all this?" She gestured at the multiple stacks of color-coded accordion folders.

Hart sobered, all business once again. "Monica heads for New York on Friday. She'll do a couple days of talk shows and print interviews there. Her European tour begins five days later. Prior to that, the itinerary all has to be vetted, from a security standpoint. Hotels, car services, the various premieres, promotional appearances."

"I had no idea so much went into it."

Hart stood and flexed the muscles in his broad shoulders. "There's a lot of work involved ahead of time to ensure that there are no issues." He grabbed his cup and ambled into the kitchen.

Maggie followed him over to the coffeemaker. "Didn't Ms. Day have a problem on a red carpet a year or so ago?"

Hart dumped the dregs in the sink. "In Cannes. A fan got past the rope lines."

"But you were right there." Maggie remembered the photos of him calmly stepping in to the rescue.

Hart rinsed his cup and refilled it. "I don't think the guy meant Monica any harm. He was just excited to see her in person. But it freaked her out, and Monica's been hypercautious ever since."

Maggie couldn't blame her. She sighed, waving off Hart's offer to get her a mug, too. Noting he had indeed eaten the last two brownies, she leaned against the counter.

"Which is why she would prefer to have me at that event."

Maggie braced her hands on either side of her. "She probably feels safe whenever you're around."

Hart put his cup down. "What makes you say that?"

Finding the cozy, low-lit kitchen—a place where they had made love—far too intimate, Maggie fled back to the dining room. While she walked, she gestured inanely. "You being ex-military and all."

"Uh-huh."

Turning, she saw Hart checking her out. "Plus, you're big and strong." *Stop now. Before you make even more of a fool of yourself.*

He grinned, as if liking what he saw. Then crossed his arms, waited, almost daring her to go on. So of course, she did.

"And you have that Don't-Mess-With-Me vibe that all confident Texas men seem to have."

One corner of his mouth crooked up. He seemed flattered. And aroused, as if he were thinking about making the moves on her again. "Good to know," he said dryly, still checking her out.

Maggie cleared her throat and got busy closing all the plantation blinds in the room. "Anyway, I'm sure Monica will miss you on this trip." When his brow furrowed, Maggie rushed on, "Because she will never feel as safe without you as she is with you."

Just as I'll never feel quite the way I do in this moment, either. Idiotic. Enamored. Half in love, and all the way in lust.

Misreading the cause behind her concern, Hart soothed, "Smitty and the rest of the security team will do fine without me."

Which then prompted the question, "Then why are you involved in the preliminary legwork when you're on leave of absence, if the rest of her team is more than qualified for the job, too?" Especially since he wasn't going on the trip?

Hart propped a shoulder against the wall and stood, sipping his coffee. "Monica's a little worried because Smitty's never been in charge of such a long or complex trip. So she wants me to go over everything. Make sure there are no potential problems. And get back to them by tomorrow morning."

Which meant he'd likely be working late into the night.

"And I'm happy to do it."

Maggie could see that. She also couldn't help but admire his strong work ethic and the concern for those around him. Couple that with his rugged good looks and the tenderness he showed in the bedroom and he was damned near the perfect man.

A perfect man she wanted more and more each day.

A perfect man who was leaving soon and taking his adorable baby son with him.

Deciding to distract herself from that, she pointed to the third container. "What's in the other box?"

He blinked at her abrupt change of subject but fortunately he did not take offense at her nosiness. A faint smile tugged at the corners of his lips. "Wrapped gifts. Baby stuff, maybe."

Maybe? "You haven't opened any of them yet?"

He regarded the box with complete disinterest, then turned back to her. "No. Why? You want to do the honors?"

Well, actually, yes. She loved opening packages and loved baby stuff even more. "You wouldn't mind?"

He chuckled. "I can see you are not going to rest until your curiosity is satisfied. Seriously, it would help me out if you would. That way I'll know what to say when Monica calls later."

Maggie dragged the box over, sat down beside him and began opening the gifts. There were half a dozen outfits from a Beverly Hills children's boutique, all perfectly sized for Henry, all of impeccable quality. And a monogrammed toddler-sized robe in blue with matching slippers. Maggie ran her fingers over the Egyptian cotton, her own longing for a baby intensifying tenfold. "This is really nice."

Hart glanced over briefly, then went back to the material he was reviewing. "Monica's got a big heart."

It seemed so. And yet, the Hollywood starlet kept sending him work, pulling him back into her world, a little bit at a time, instead of supporting his need to be with his son.

"You think she's going to be okay with the

adjustments you're going to need to make to your schedule now that you're a dad?"

"She has been so far." Hart kept working. "It'll be fine."

Maggie hoped so.

He tilted his head. "Of course, if you're worried," he quipped lightly, seduction in his eyes, "you could always come with us to California."

As what? A friend? A mistress? Nanny? None of those options appealed to her.

Maggie wet her lips. "I thought you wanted me to stay here and run the wedding ranch business while your parents went with you."

Hart's eyes darkened. "That was option number two. My first choice has always been to have you with me—and Henry."

And though the idea of being with them was appealing, the thought of leaving her entire life behind to play house in California, for an unspecified amount of time, was not.

If Maggie was going to consider engaging in more than friendship with Hart, she would need a sign that he was willing to sacrifice for her, too.

"Or you could take a real leave of absence from your job and stay here," she offered, mimicking his casual tone. "Hang out at the ranch for a while. Get to know your son. Help your parents get The Wedding Train business back on track and/or transition into at least semi-retirement."

Which would then, in turn, also give the two of them time to explore whatever this was that was blossoming between them.

His expression turned brooding. "You're right. I do need to have a better business revitalization plan for my folks when I talk to them before I leave. Do you think Callie would be willing to work something up for them to peruse, ASAP?"

The thought of steering more work to her sister, who had been freelancing since Brian's birth, was appealing. "I can certainly ask her."

Half an hour later, she was able to report back

to him. "Callie can pull something together on short notice, but she's going to need to come to the ranch, have a look around, maybe stay a few days in order to adequately craft a social media solution."

Hart leaned back in his chair as he mulled that over. "What about her son?"

"She would have to bring him with her. Will that be a problem?"

"Not at all. In fact, to make things easier, she and her little boy should stay here at the ranch with us."

Then they'd have two tiny chaperones and the ultimate cheerleader of romance. That ought to make life interesting. Maggie smiled. "I'll let her know."

"Sounds good." Hart caught her wrist, and his gaze roved over her in a way that made her think her father hadn't scared him off, after all.

"And Maggie?" he said quietly, reeling her in. His thumb tenderly stroked the inside of her wrist. "Thanks for helping out. Henry and

I couldn't have gotten through the last week without you."

"You're welcome," Maggie said softly.

The trouble was, she wanted a lot more than gratitude from him. More than sex and friendship. She wanted love.

Chapter Eleven

Hart was already in the kitchen the next morning, making breakfast and talking on the phone, when Maggie walked in. It was the same scene that had played out nearly every morning since he'd been in residence at the ranch, yet she never got used to seeing him in such a cozy domestic setting.

The epitome of masculine sexiness, he was clad in pajamas and T-shirt, his hair tousled, morning beard lining his handsome face.

The long, encompassing look and warm, welcoming smile he gave her made her heart take another small, telltale leap.

As much as she wanted to deny it, there was something growing between them. The fact that she wished the night before had ended with a kiss, and more lovemaking, instead of endless business calls on his part was really a moot point. They had needed to slow down and reflect, and they had. Where they went from here remained to be seen.

In the meantime, she could do what Hart advised and enjoy the moment.

Seeing her, Henry waved at her enthusiastically from his high chair. Maggie walked over to greet him. Generous as ever, the little boy offered her a bite of the breakfast his daddy had made for him.

"Mmm," she said softly, swallowing the syrup-dipped French toast. "That's good."

Henry chortled and stuffed another buttery golden brown square in his mouth.

Still listening to whomever was talking on the other end of the connection, Hart gestured for her to help herself. "It's going to be fine,

Smitty." He poured her some coffee while she transferred two slices of perfectly prepared French toast onto her plate. "I have a few suggestions to help make things run a little more smoothly and will email them to you later this morning. But overall, everything you and the rest of the team have done thus far looks pretty good."

Hart paused. "Yeah. I know she wishes I were around to handle this." Another moment of silence. "She knows I'll be back on the job by the time you all get back from Europe. And I'll be available to do anything I can, long-distance, while you're there."

Hart concluded the call. Then he filled a plate for himself and joined her at the breakfast table.

The coziness factor in the room increased tenfold. If only, Maggie thought wistfully, the three of them could remain suspended in this time without the rest of the world ever crowding in.

His gaze roved over her warmly, as if he were mentally calculating when and where they could next make love. "What time is Callie coming over?"

Maggie smiled. "Around eleven."

Briefly, he covered her hand with his. "Any chance you could spell me with Henry long enough for me to grab a shower?"

Ignoring the heat the contact generated, Maggie tried not to drown in the molten brown depths of his eyes. "No problem."

"Thanks. I was going to try and put him in his crib with his stuffed animals." Hart shot his son a wry look. "Then I caught him trying to throw a leg over the rail this morning."

Imagining how it would hurt to hit the wood floor, Maggie said, "Oh, dear."

"Fortunately, he didn't seem to have figured out the logistics of escaping his crib just yet. But it won't be long before he's off and running free."

Like father like son, Maggie thought, *he's*

restless to the core. She sat back slightly to survey them both. "He likes to be on the move."

Hart sent her a sidelong glance. "Anyway, thanks for watching him," he said in a voice that was so soft and husky it brought forth an answering well of tenderness in Maggie. "I won't take long."

Maggie sipped coffee. "No worries. Take all the time you need."

Hart rose. Before he had finished putting his dishes in the dishwasher, his phone rang again. He glanced at the caller ID and immediately picked up. "Yeah. Thanks for calling back so quickly. I'm going to need at least a two bedroom, two bath. As soon as possible. I'm okay with staying in the same building, but if your company has a unit closer to where I work, one that's a little more family-friendly, that would be even better…."

He smiled and waved at them both, still listening, then walked out, already moving on.

Which was, Maggie told herself firmly, what she should be doing, too. If she were smart.

Trouble was, where Hart Sanders was concerned, she wasn't sure she wanted to walk away.

LUCKILY FOR MAGGIE, Callie and Brian arrived at the Double Knot several hours later. With Hart involved in yet another phone conference with "the team," Maggie and Henry gave Callie and her son, Brian, a tour of the property. Then she and Callie retreated to the Double Knot offices to finish the initial consultation and transfer of information, while the two little boys played together in the small playroom just off Maggie's office.

Callie, whose own dark chocolate curls had been cut at chin length since her son's birth, looked around admiringly. "The set-up here is ideal if you have small children."

Maggie got up to retrieve a ball that had become lodged beneath the sofa. When she returned it to the little ones, Henry brought her down to eye level and kissed her cheek. Maggie embraced him back, gave her nephew the same hug and kiss, then went back to join her sister. "Apparently, Hart used to play there as a child when his parents were working. Frank and Fiona kept it for clients after that."

Callie nodded approvingly. "Henry and Brian are sure loving it. In fact, Henry seems to have become enormously attached to you, too."

"So true," Maggie rasped out. And it went both ways. She loved Henry, too. Without warning, tears pressed against the backs of her eyes.

Callie embraced her in a fierce, sisterly hug. "It's going to kill you when he leaves, isn't it?"

Maggie drew a deep breath and waved away the tears. "I'm just hormonal or something," she lied.

Callie scoffed, clearly worried now. "Or something, all right. I saw the way you and Hart were looking at each other before he got on that last call. I mean, I already knew from what you haven't said and what Mom and Dad did say…"

Maggie tensed and reached for a tissue. "What was that?"

"The usual. They're worried you're letting someone else dictate priorities for you again."

When in truth, Maggie thought, it was the opposite. Being with Hart, finding out just how vulnerable she was, was a wake-up call she could not ignore.

She squared her shoulders. "I know I have to move on," she said honestly. "And the first thing I want is a family. So I started exploring my options."

Maggie went to her desk and pulled a folder out of the bottom drawer. She handed it over to Callie.

Her twin frowned. "What happened to the old-fashioned way? Dating. Falling in love. Getting married."

"I tried all that and failed. Miserably."

"So start dating that handsome hunk of burning love who only appears to have eyes for you."

"Come on, Callie. You know I can't date him."

"Why not? He's male, single…and mighty attractive."

Boy, was he ever. Abruptly, Maggie felt like crying again. "He's also headed back to California the first chance he gets." *Adorable son in tow.*

"That is where he works."

"I can't give up everything I have here just because I find him attractive."

Callie kicked back in her chair, clearly exasperated. "I thought you wanted to move on with your life."

Maggie did. But…She shook her head, angry now with her sister, circumstances, the world. "You just don't understand."

Callie released an aggrieved sigh. "What it's like to feel like you're in an incredible rut and have no way to get out? Yet you know if you don't do something soon you really will go into a tailspin?"

The hurt and frustration in her sister's tone had Maggie blinking. "You're feeling the same thing?"

Callie laughed wanly and buried her head in her hands. "Even when we're miles apart, we're always on the same page emotionally. Don't you know that?"

Maggie stared at her identical twin, aware that even when life had them on separate paths they always ended up in sync. She had just hoped that in this instance their outcomes would have been different. "I thought—despite losing Seth so unexpectedly—that you had found a way to be happy again."

Callie straightened, courageous as ever. "I am happy in terms of being a mother. The rest of it—living in Laramie…being the tragic figure of Seth's widow—is suffocating me."

Maggie had been so wrapped up in her own

problems, she hadn't paid attention to Callie's. "What are you going to do?"

"Same as you." Callie drew a deep breath and looked Maggie right in the eye. "Figure a way out. And soon."

"So what do you think?" Hart asked, late that evening, when Callie and Maggie emerged from her Double Knot office and joined him in the living room. "Do you have enough to pull together a sample video campaign for the ranch before my parents get back from Australia four days from now?"

Upstairs, the boys were still sleeping peacefully. Which was no surprise. They'd had a great day together and had both gone down without protest after dinner and bath. The blessed silence that reverberated through the house meant the adults could focus on ironing out all the business details without any distractions.

"Well…?" Hart prodded. "Don't keep me in suspense."

Callie shook her head, exasperated by Hart's demanding nature almost as much as Maggie was. "You don't ask much, do you?"

He flashed a cocky grin at her twin. "Never."

Callie slipped back into business mode. "I can put together a video compilation and set it to some popular wedding music. It would help a lot, though, if you and Maggie took some video footage of the wedding setup without guests. Photos of the interiors of the train, the scenery you will see during the ride up the mountain, what it looks like at Nature's Cathedral, with at least a dozen folding chairs and the flower strewn arbor that serves as the altar." She furrowed her brow. "Also take video of the dance floor, the stage for the band and the set tables in the reception hall. The circular drive, where the bride and groom will ride off into the sunset via stretch limousine is nice, too."

Callie smiled as Hart paid close attention. "Providing the background will allow prospective brides and grooms to imagine themselves getting married there."

Hart nodded enthusiastically. "My parents are going to love this."

Callie sobered. "I'll also talk to the tech guys I use and devise a plan for burying some of the negative reviews a lot further down on the major internet search engines. All that will help."

Hart smiled. "Sure you don't want a full-time job here?" he teased. "Since Maggie's planning to leave?"

Callie hesitated, showing Maggie how intrigued her twin was by the idea. But when Callie responded to Hart, it was with a staying palm. "First things first. Let's see if we can't talk your parents into taking the Double Knot ranch and The Wedding Train out of the doldrums and into the future...."

To HART'S RELIEF, by the time Callie and Brian left after breakfast the next morning, Pete and his wife had arrived ready to work. While Pete got the steam train cranked up, Marisol set up tables in the reception barn for both rehearsal and bridal dinners. Maggie brought the bridal limousine around and parked it in the drive. Wanting to get this done while Henry was still in a cooperative mood, Hart settled Henry in his stroller, got the video camera set and turned to Maggie.

In deference to the heat of the summer day, Maggie had swept her curls on top of her head in a loose, sexy knot. She looked pretty and relaxed in a pair of white figure-hugging jeans and a sleeveless coral blouse. She'd also pulled on sensible western boots, perfect for traipsing around some of the wilder areas of the ranch.

He wanted her in the worst way—but remained determined to follow her cues and let them slow down. At least until he had the easier areas of his life settled.

As their eyes met, he asked, "How about we do everything at the lower elevation first and then head up to Nature's Cathedral last?"

Maggie smiled. "Sounds good to me," she said in a soft, sultry voice that stirred his senses even more.

Fortunately, Henry was a trouper throughout the event-filled morning. By lunchtime, however, his son had clearly had his fill, so Maggie and Hart took him into the kitchen where they all had lunch. No sooner had he finished than he was yawning and beginning to fuss. Maggie tidied up the kitchen, while Hart took Henry upstairs for a diaper change. Henry wasn't exactly cooperative. By the time they'd finished, Maggie had joined them in the nursery.

"So what do you think?" he asked softly, as they exchanged smiles. He inclined his head toward his son, who was jumping up and down on his crib mattress, like a kangaroo on a rampage. "Do you think we could put him in his car seat long enough to get the Nature's Cathedral shots done?"

Confident as ever when it came to caring for children, Maggie plucked several of Henry's small stuffed animals from the crib. "As long as these go along for the ride, I think we'll be okay."

Henry had other ideas. He yelled and arched his back the moment he was put in the car seat.

Maggie dashed into the ranch house and returned with the rest of his seven stuffed animals. Henry promptly threw out all but the zebra and the blanket.

Hart slid behind the wheel of the ranch pickup truck. "Well, what do you know," he drawled, in a vain attempt to find humor in the situation. "Do you think he finally picked just one?"

They locked eyes and Maggie chuckled at the joke. Henry yelled again and reached for the animals he had just thrown out.

Maggie placed them back in the seat with him.

Henry sighed. Loudly.

Yet, to everyone's relief, before they'd gone a quarter mile up the old logging road that led to the top of Sanders Mountain, Henry was fast asleep.

Hart reached the plateau that had formed at the peak. Wordlessly, he set the brake, put all four windows down, cut the motor. The soothing sounds of nature filled the interior, the birdsong and breeze sifting through the trees better than any sleep-inducing noise machine.

Hart reached for the video recorder and took footage of his sleeping child, then turned the camera to Maggie and filmed her, too.

He'd never been a sentimental guy. Until now. But this was a Hallmark card moment, come to life.

Maggie looked at him, a question in her eyes.

Unaccustomed emotion stirring in his chest, Hart gazed back at her a long time, not sure how to put all he was feeling into words. Finally, he said, his voice inexplicably gruff, "Some moments you just want to remember."

He leaned across the bench seat and pressed a kiss to her temple. His pulse quickened as she melted against him. "This is one of them."

And, if luck was with him, the first of many more to come.

EVERY TIME MAGGIE thought Hart could no longer surprise her, he did something that made her forgo reality and hope for the impossible.

This was one of those times. Especially since he was looking at her like he wanted a lot more than a simple fling. But whether that would be enough to keep her happy, she did not know.

They still had a job to do, so she carefully eased from the pickup, leaving Hart to follow. He came up behind her, video camera in hand.

Pete had already set up the latticework arbor that served as the altar in Nature's Cathedral. As Maggie approached it, she was transported back to the fateful day she had first interacted with Hart. She had known he was watching her as she came up the aisle on her father's arm.

She had also realized that he knew just how scared she was of making a mistake.

Hart paused at her elbow and studied her expression. "You okay?"

Maggie pushed the image of a tuxedo-clad Hart, standing next to her at the latticework arbor, away. She did not need to be thinking about what it would be like to marry him.

"Yes. Just tired." *Tired of pretending I'm not falling head over heels in love with you.* He set down the camera, wrapped an arm around her shoulders and pulled her in close so she was nestled against his side. It was the first time he'd held her since they'd last kissed. She luxuriated in the heat of his body and the desire in his eyes.

"Maybe we should take a break then," he murmured.

And maybe, Maggie thought suddenly, "a break" was the last thing they should be taking.

She drew a deep breath and turned to face him. Why was she pretending she was okay without him? During the past two years, she had spent all her time and energy trying to make up for her mistakes. Too scared to make new ones, she had led a cloistered existence, helping others take the giant leap of faith into marriage, but daring nothing for herself.

Being there with Hart and his son made her want to change all that. It made her want her own family. Her own life. And especially her own happily-ever-after.

"What are you thinking?" he asked softly.

Maggie looked up at him. "How glad I am I didn't tie the knot that day." And she was even more elated that he had been the one who had rescued her in the woods.

"Because you wouldn't have been happy?"

"Because," Maggie said, "if I had, I never would have gotten to know you."

His eyes darkened. He threaded his hand through her hair, then fastened his lips on hers in a riveting kiss that stole her breath. The hardness of his chest pressed against her breasts. Lower still, she could feel the rigid proof of his desire. She arched against him, wanting and needing so much more, yet knowing it wasn't the time. Or the place, in the middle of a clearing, with Henry sleeping in the car, just a short distance away.

She splayed her hands across his chest and struggled to get her feelings under control. "I'm glad you're my friend, Hart."

His mouth took on a rueful twist at her description of what they were to each other, but there was no disguising the passion in his eyes. He slid a hand down her spine, brought it lazily around to cup her breast. A thrill shot through her and her nipple grew taut against his palm. He dropped a soft kiss on her temple, the shell of her ear, the sensitive spot on the nape of her neck.

"Then as such, you ought to know," he whispered, still caressing her gently, "I want to be much, much more than friends."

Hope rising within her, she read the sensual

promise in his dark brown eyes. "Friends with benefits," she guessed, for the first time allowing herself to think that maybe the whole long-distance thing could work…if he went back to California…because, as Callie had pointed out, that was where his job was.

Seeming at last to be on the same page with her, Hart bent his head and kissed her again, deeply, evocatively. "Friends with benefits and much, much more."

Chapter Twelve

Hart knew it was no time to be proposing they take this to the next level when he was still trying to get a solution worked out behind the scenes. Yet his intent—to make her his woman—was the same.

Henry had other ideas.

Awakening to find himself in his car seat—alone—he let out a yowl loud enough to wake every bird in the forest. It didn't matter that Maggie and Hart both were back at the pickup truck in fifteen seconds flat to reassure him.

His son was mad. And he let them know it.

Murmuring all the while, Hart disengaged

the safety straps. He lifted his son out of the car seat. Henry kicked him in the ribs, whacked him in the face with his elbow and cried some more.

Hart's gut twisted at the sound.

Henry was as upset as he had been the day Hart had picked him up from social services. And it didn't matter what he did or said, his son wanted nothing to do with him.

Henry wanted Maggie.

Looking as teary-eyed as Hart felt over his inability to adequately soothe his child, Maggie took Henry in her arms.

"Mommy. Mommy. Mommy...." Henry cried, clinging to her all the tighter.

And finally Maggie cried, too.

Hart was so damned overcome, so useless in the situation to comfort either one of them, so helpless against the guilt and the sorrow churning in his gut for having unwittingly abandoned his child and causing this situation, he did the only thing he could and walked away to the edge of the clearing.

As his tears flowed, Henry's eventually ebbed. By the time Hart got a hold of himself and walked back, Maggie looked composed, too.

"I guess it was a bad idea to leave him in the car without one of us there," she said, cuddling his now-contented son close. "Even though we were less than twenty feet away, in plain view, he probably thought we had abandoned him."

"We won't make the mistake again," Hart vowed. One way or another, he was going to find a way to keep Maggie in their lives. He owed it to them all.

NOT SURPRISINGLY, HENRY was hard to put down that evening. Hart rocked him for a very long time. When his son was finally asleep, he returned several of the business calls he had missed. None were pleasant. It seemed he was letting everyone down today.

Relieved to have business over with, nevertheless, he went in search of Maggie. He finally found her curled up on the chaise lounge in her bedroom. She had recently showered and changed into a pair of pink plaid pajama pants, white tank top, and pink cotton cardigan. Her feet were bare, her toenails painted a pretty pink. She had her dark curls swept up on top of her head, a cup of hot tea beside her and a manila folder in her hand.

Hart sauntered closer and looked down to see what she was reading. He sank down on the edge of the chaise. "You're serious about artificial insemination?" he asked, stunned.

She looked over at him, her expression determined. "I told you I've been thinking about having a baby on my own."

Hart wasn't surprised Maggie wanted a child. However, it frustrated him to find her shortchanging herself yet again. "Isn't *making* a baby half the fun?"

Her lips curved ruefully as his joke hit home.

"In your case, probably. In mine," she pointed to the typed list of all the scientific ways to procreate, "maybe not so much."

To Hart's mounting despair, she really seemed to believe it.

Was this the opening he had been looking for? The way to convince Maggie to throw her future in with theirs? "If you want a baby, there are better ways to have one."

She put down her papers. "Such as?"

Knowing what a great mom she would be by the magic she worked with Henry, he said, "With a husband, or lover."

A smile bloomed on her pretty face. "Except I'm not really the marrying kind, thus far," she pointed out, humor glinting in her eyes. "And my biological clock is ticking louder than ever."

"Because of Callie and Brian, the fact the two of you have done everything together?" he interjected curiously.

She picked up her papers again, then let them fall to her lap.

"I admit we always wanted to raise our children together. It just didn't work out that way. But being with Callie and the two boys today gave me a glimpse of what it would be like if we ever did have children at the same time. And it sent my baby fever into high gear." She sighed wistfully. "So…I'm looking at options."

"It makes sense, but I still think you deserve more."

Maggie shrugged and stood. "Don't we all?" she said thickly.

Hart rose and took her in his arms. "Hey," he said, threading his hands through her hair and tilting her face up to his. "Don't sell yourself short," he whispered. And then he did what he had been wanting to do again all day. He brought her close and kissed her with every fiber of his being.

ALTHOUGH MAGGIE HAD pretended she could be satisfied just hanging out with Hart—as friends with benefits—she had known, deep in her heart, that wasn't true. She wanted so much more from their relationship.

She wanted to know she could count on Hart to be there whenever, however she needed him. She wanted them to mean the world to each other. And as she opened her mouth to the plundering heat of his and recklessly let herself yield, she began to think that her dreams just might come true.

She moaned softly as he clasped her to him and deepened the kiss until it was so wild and reckless it stole her breath. Unable to turn away from his raw aching need, she savored the feel of his powerful chest against her breasts and the comfort and safety of being cradled in his strong arms. Lower still, his hardness elicited a whole new sling of tingles.

For too long she had let herself believe she could keep her guard up and be happy alone. Hart made her feel that the future was theirs for the taking, that they had always been slated to be together. All she had to do was muster the courage to expand her horizons and see where the future led.

And that wasn't hard to do as he eased his hands beneath her camisole pajama top, gently caressing her ribs, before moving upward to tenderly cup her breasts. Her nipples grew taut. And then his mouth was on her flesh, creating a frenzy of wanting.

Her fingers fell to the waistband of his jeans, but he was kneeling, easing off the rest of her clothes. Laying her back on the chaise, he touched and kissed her until sensation swept over her in great enervating waves and she came apart in his hands.

And then it was her turn, to rise and slowly undress him. Looking her fill. Touching and kissing everywhere, too. Liking the fact he was willing to let her set the pace, she guided him over to her bed and stretched out beside him in the sheets. He was all warm satin skin and firm, hard muscle.

She rolled him onto his back and lay beside

him, kissing him, caressing him with her hand, until his ridge of arousal grew ever harder, and he was throbbing every bit as much as she was. Feeling sexier and more adventurous than she ever had in her life, she draped her body over his. Kissed him again, sliding even lower, driving him to the brink in return.

And then they were switching places once again. He rolled her onto her back, captured her wrists in his hands and drew them above her head. She lay beneath him, captive to whatever he wanted. And what he wanted, she soon discovered, was to take possession with earth-shattering skill and tenderness. Still letting her know how much she deserved, how much he wanted her to have, he pressed into her as deeply as he could. She rose to meet him, savoring his heat and hardness.

Again and again, they kissed, their mouths mating every bit as intensely as the rest of their bodies. Slowly, steadily, his incredibly erotic possession built. Until there was no more holding back. No more pretending they did not need each other as intensely as they needed this. Together, they went soaring into bliss. Tenderly, inevitably, they came back down.

HART LAY BESIDE Maggie in the pale light of her bedroom, happier than he had been in a long time. Maybe because he had the most amazing woman he had ever known clasped against him. And maybe because he sensed that although she was falling as hard and fast for him as he was for her, he was still a long way from closing the deal.

Had to be if she was even looking at having a baby with a stranger in a very scientific way.

But that could be fixed with enough time and effort and tender loving care. After all, look what they had already managed in just a week and a half. Who knew what would happen in a month, a year…a lifetime?

Geared up to make her happier than she had

ever been, he pressed a kiss into the fragrant softness of her hair. Nuzzled close. "Round two?"

Her gentle laughter was music to his ears.

Maggie facetiously threw her forearm across her brow. "Hart Sanders," she chided. "You are going to wear me out."

He grinned, rolled onto his back and brought her on top of him. Enjoying the soft silky warmth of her, he traced the enticing womanly curve of her derriere, then clasped her close. "I'm sure working on it."

She shivered as he found one of her many sweet spots. "Well, you know what they say," she teased.

He found another. Was rewarded by the hardening of her nipples rubbing against his chest. "If at first you don't succeed…"

Hart kissed the nape of her neck.

Maggie kissed back and found a few of his own sweet spots. "Try. Try again…"

They did. And it was one hell of a euphorically satisfying night.

A sign of the bliss yet to come.

THE SUN WAS just peeking through the blinds when the sound of Henry starting to wake came through on the baby monitor. Maggie slipped from the bed and went in to get him. The tyke was lying on his back, stuffed animals tucked all around him. He had the hem of his blanket clenched in one fist. Seeing her, he scrambled to his feet, the difficulties of the day before apparently forgotten. "Mommy, Mommy, Mommy!" he said, hugging her close.

"Maggie, Maggie, Maggie," she said in return, lifting him up all the way.

Henry shook his head. "*Mommy*," he declared.

Hart appeared in the doorway, clad in a pair of low slung pajama pants and the usual T-shirt. He had a day's growth of beard lining his jaw, a serious case of bed head and a sleek muscled body that would put a Calvin Klein underwear model to shame. He strolled closer with the look of a man who had been very well loved and her heart leapt at the sight of him. Hart laid a kiss on Maggie's head, then reached for his son and did the same. "I agree, bucko," Hart said, cuddling the two of them close. "Maggie would make a wonderful mommy."

She blushed. "The here and now, remember?"

Hart kissed her sweetly. "Sounds good to me."

Reluctantly, Maggie transferred Henry to Hart, along with a clean diaper. "How about you do the honors, while I make breakfast this morning?" It was only fair, since he had taken the majority of the kitchen duty thus far.

Hart smiled. "Be right down."

Maggie had just gotten the skillet out and set it on the stove when a shiny black SUV drove up the lane and parked in front of the house. A uniformed driver got out and opened the rear passenger door. A gorgeous redhead emerged just as Hart came down the stairs and into the kitchen, and they watched as she started down the path that led to the front door.

"That's Monica Day!" Maggie breathed. The actress was even more stunningly beautiful in person than on film.

Hart nodded. He did not look particularly pleased to see his boss.

"Did you know she was coming?"

Again, he shook his head. Henry still in his arms, Hart opened the back door and walked out. Monica saw them, spun around and strode toward father and son. She greeted Henry warmly. The little boy smiled back. The two adults talked a little more. Finally, Hart turned and headed back for the house, Monica Day gliding gracefully beside him.

Acutely aware she was still in her pajamas, Maggie touched a hand to her hair. Had she even combed it? She couldn't remember.

Hart made introductions. "Maggie, this is my

boss, Monica Day. Monica, our—" he hesitated slightly "—friend Maggie McCabe."

Well, they *were* friends, weren't they?

At least he hadn't said "lover."

Or "friends with benefits."

"Nice to meet you," Monica said, as cordially as if Maggie hadn't been standing there clearly fresh from a night of wild lovemaking.

"Would you mind taking Henry upstairs while Monica and I talk?" Hart asked, genially.

"Sure thing." Maggie grabbed a box of dry cereal and juice for Henry's breakfast and slipped out. She and Henry went up the stairs to her room, so Maggie could get dressed.

Had Hart and his guest stayed in the kitchen, Maggie would not have been able to hear what was being said. However, Hart and his boss had moved to the living room, directly below Maggie's bedroom.

Monica's elegant voice projected clearly up the staircase. "I admit, I don't have kids, so I don't know exactly how you feel, Hart. However, I can certainly see what an adorable little boy your Henry is. How much you love him already. And I empathize with your predicament…"

"I've missed so much of his life already…I have to be with him."

Monica seemed to understand that. Then her voice rose once again. "Look, I know you, remember? I know how restless you get if you're in one place for even a few weeks, Hart."

More of him dissenting.

Then Monica promising, "…accommodations. And in return…"

Eventually, the voices moved outside. Car doors opened and shut.

The shiny black SUV started up and drove off. A minute later, Hart walked upstairs and joined Maggie in her room. She knew immediately from the look on his face that a lot had transpired in her absence. As calmly as possible, she asked, "What's going on?"

"The studio added a ninth country to Monica's European publicity tour. She doesn't think Smitty can handle it. She wants me to go with her."

Maggie stared at him in shock. "And you're considering it?"

His expression remained inscrutable. "It's my job."

Maggie felt pressure building behind her eyes. "What about Henry?"

"I can take him with me."

Really? The child who had already been through so much. The child who had become hysterical when in a car seat not twenty feet from and in plain sight of them both. A child who sometimes took a lot to comfort.

Hart caught her skeptical glance. "There's a nanny agency in Beverly Hills. They specialize in helping families who wish to travel or work abroad. It'll be fine," he said bluntly.

And the trouble was, Maggie realized, so disappointed in Hart she could barely speak, he really seemed to believe that.

HART HAD HOPED Maggie would see how much he and Henry needed her and that she'd volunteer to travel with them. Instead, he watched with unbelievable disappointment as she emotionally withdrew.

Standing stiff as a statue, she watched Henry make another foray into her closet, peek around the frame and then go back in.

Her face pale, she flashed a wan smile. "I really should get a shower. The caterer, florist and musicians for the Randolph-Albertson wedding are going to be here at ten to discuss setup and go over the final details for the reception."

Hart glanced at his watch, saw how late it was. "And I promised my parents I'd call them on Skype. Henry and I will do that now."

Unfortunately, his son was in no mind to cooperate. He couldn't stay on Hart's lap and in front of the computer camera for more than two seconds at a time. The rest of the time, he was hankering to get down and run wild and free.

"Like father, like son," Frank chuckled. "Probably restless from the day he was born."

Hart's mom agreed. "He really is the spitting image of you at that age, honey. We can't wait to hold him."

Speaking of which…Hart set the squirming Henry down and watched him run off to play with his toys. He didn't know how much time he had so he cut straight to the chase. "Did you get my email?"

His mom and dad exchanged tentative glances. "We did," his dad said.

Hart sensed bad news coming.

Fiona took a deep breath. "First of all, Hart, please don't petition Maggie into staying on at the Double Knot any longer than she feels comfortable. She's been living one day, one month at a time since her marriage plans went bust, and any undue pressure from you to make a long term commitment she may or may not be ready for might set her back."

Hart would not have believed that while making love to her the night before. Now, in the wake of his "news," he wasn't so sure.

"Of course we'll come out to California to visit you and Henry whenever we can," his mom continued. "But we can't just pick up and move out there."

Hart stared at them.

First Maggie defecting. Now them? "It wouldn't have to be forever," he said. "If Maggie doesn't want to stay on at the Double Knot, then we'll find someone else to run the ranch—" *like her sister Callie* "—or you can just come back here eventually and take over again."

"We know you need help with Henry making the adjustment to life with you in Los Angeles. But honestly—"

"I understand if you want your own place," Hart cut in. "And I've already thought this all through. I'll buy you a house nearby or rent you an apartment in our building."

Frank shook his head, "It's not that, son.

Texas is our home. We don't want to live any-where else."

Hart took a moment to consider the irony. He had always been the one to leave. Now his parents were walking out on him. "So, in other words, you can't help me and Henry out. Even for a few months," he reiterated, unbearably hurt.

Again, Frank and Fiona exchanged looks. But this time they were clearly of one mind, one heart. "We'll do everything we can within reason," his mom said. "But unless you move back to Texas," his dad stipulated firmly, "we won't be able to help you with Henry on a daily basis."

HART SPENT THE rest of the day caring for Henry and interviewing traveling nannies via phone while Maggie worked with the staff on the setup for the Randolph-Albertson wed-ding. By the time she walked in the door a lit-tle after 8 p.m., Henry was already fed, bathed and sleeping peacefully. Hart, meanwhile, was just trying to decide what he wanted for dinner that did not require any effort.

Maggie slipped off her shoes. She left them on the mat by the door and walked barefoot to the fridge. "Problem?"

Hart had never known that skirts that ended just above the knee could be so darned sexy. Or that a sleeveless blouse, partially untucked, could have him itching to pull it all the way out. And off...

Maggie waited, brow lifted in anticipation.

Hart cleared his throat. "Just wishing there were something closer," he said honestly. "So we could order take-out delivered." He paused to study the new blush of sun across her cheeks and nose. "Don't you ever get stir-crazy, living all the way out here? So far from everything?"

"Hankering for some night life?"

"Something," Hart acknowledged with a shrug. *Like a yes from you. Yes to Europe. Yes to California. Yes to being with me from now on out. Yes to no more running away...*

Clearly misreading the reason behind his private musing, Maggie used her hip to lightly nudge him aside. "I've never been much of a party person, even in college. For me a satisfying night is a nice dinner—which we're about to have—some pleasant company or something entertaining to watch on TV." She reached into the fridge and brought out a nice bottle of wine, a hunk of cheddar, a bowl of fresh fruit and some artisan bread.

She studied his expression while handing him the bottle opener. "Obviously," she teased, "I have just shocked and dismayed you."

She was certainly in a better mood.

Maybe he should be, too.

So Hart followed his own advice to Maggie and took the opportunity to appreciate the moment they were in. Which was, as it happened, pretty damned enticing.

A quiet night in Texas.

The ranch house to themselves.

The baby asleep upstairs.

A bottle of wine to share.

He smiled and playfully tugged on a lock of her hair. "Actually, what you just described sounds awfully good to me after a day of corralling Henry. Who, by the way, has more juice in him than the Energizer Bunny."

"He can be a live wire." Maggie arranged grapes, fresh peach slices and mango on a plate. "What did your parents think of him?"

Hart poured two glasses of wine. "How many ways can you say adorable?" he quipped. "They're counting the minutes until they get home to see us."

"I'll bet," Maggie murmured, adding the cheese and bread to a plate. Together, they carried everything into the living room. They settled on the sofa, with the dinner tray on the coffee table in front of them. "What else did they say?"

Briefly, Hart explained his folks' refusal to

help him out. He studied her expression. Was he the only one without a clue? "You don't look surprised."

She inclined her head. "They love this ranch. Of course they don't want to live anywhere but Sanders Mountain." She paused. "I am glad they're willing to look at a proposal from Callie, though. Bringing Nature's Cathedral and The Wedding Train into the world of social media could make the Double Knot Wedding Ranch a huge draw as a destination wedding again."

That would be good.

"Plus, it doesn't hurt that you're finally getting involved in the family business, the way they have always wanted, even if it is only as part owner and investor." She sipped her wine and peered at him playfully, "Now if you would just love the Lone Star State as much as the rest of us do."

He laid a palm over his heart. "Hey, I love it here, too." Always had.

"And yet," she silently toasted him with her glass, before taking another slow sip, "you are always hankering to leave."

He facetiously narrowed his gaze. "Always hankering to explore new things."

A brief silence fell. She broke a few plump green grapes off the stem and handed them to him. "So you never miss it?"

He munched them gratefully, then cut up some cheese. "I didn't say that. I miss some things."

She smiled and kept her gaze level with his. "Like what?"

He shrugged and tore off several hunks of the crusty bread. "Tex-Mex food."

"Of course."

"Barbecue." Their smiles clashed.

"Only food?" she teased.

He went on, revealing his long list of favorite Texas things. "The big blue skies. The wide open spaces. The big hearts of the people."

A deeply sentimental expression crossed her lovely face. "I love all those things, too."

Now he knew what the problem was. "So, you don't ever want to leave Texas," he said, a little sadly.

"Now, now." She turned to face him, her bent knee nudging his thigh. "Don't make assumptions. I'm not one of those people who have never left the state. Although, to be fair, one can travel broadly within Texas without ever leaving the borders, given how large an area it encompasses."

Admiring the turquoise pendant nestled in the notch collar of her blouse, just above her breasts, Hart asked, "Where have you been?"

Heightened color swept her elegant cheekbones. "Lots of places. D.C. New Orleans. Florida. New York City. Paris. London."

He squinted, not sure if she was pulling his leg or not. "Paris, Texas, or Paris, France?"

Another droll look. "Paris, France. And don't

ask if it's London, Kentucky, or London, England. You know it's the latter."

He grinned. So she was more cosmopolitan than she usually let on. "When?"

Maggie propped an elbow on the sofa cushion behind her. "While I was in college. I went with one of the families I nannied for."

This was news. Why hadn't she mentioned it earlier? Unless, as his parents supposed, it was because she was still reeling from her previous mistake. And did not want to be put in a position where she could be pushed to do anything she did not want to do again.

He tucked a lock of hair behind her ear. "What did you think?"

Maggie went very still. "Honestly? That it wasn't the best place to take a child, at least for a two-week-long vacation. The time change was brutal. Both kids were really out of sorts and off schedule the whole time, which made the sightseeing the parents wanted to do challenging, to say the least."

Or, in other words, Hart thought, they'd all been miserable. Still…Different people, different situation. He took her wrist in hand and rubbed his thumb over her jumping pulse. "You've never wanted to go back? Enjoy the continent under more pleasurable circumstances?" He could certainly envision being there with her.

"I do," Maggie admitted readily. "But it seems like I'm always saving up for something." She reached for the bottle of wine and topped off both their glasses. "What about you?" She paused to study him. "Have you traveled there for fun? Or is it always just for work?"

"Work. But one day…"

She laughed, the sound soft and musical. She waggled a teasing brow. "Or, in other words, you are no better at taking vacations than I am."

He warmed under her all-seeing gaze. "Could change."

"Could."

They exchanged quiet smiles.

And Hart knew, once again, they were on the verge. "The question is," he said, reaching over to smooth the hair from her face, "will we?"

Chapter Thirteen

"Actually," Maggie said, not quite looking Hart in the eye. She extricated herself from his light embrace, rose with graceful ease, and carried the remnants of their dinner to the kitchen. "I already am making some changes."

He followed, with the wine glasses and quarter-full bottle of zinfandel. "Such as?" He watched her put the leftover cheese and fruit away.

Maggie turned on the faucet and rinsed her hands. "I've decided to move up my timetable a little, and go ahead and find another job. I contacted a head-hunting firm that specializes in business analyst jobs."

Hart studied her defiantly nonchalant expression. Was it his imagination or was she beginning to look a little bit conflicted again? In any case, there was one thing he had to know. He braced his hands on either side of her. "Did you do this before or after I met with Monica today?"

She sighed and tipped her face up to his. "Does it matter?" When he did not reply, she pushed on, "You know this has been my plan. Just as yours has been to go back to California." Splaying a hand across his chest, she moved him out of her path.

With a shrug, she headed for the laundry room.

"Now with your parents returning to Texas, Callie presenting them with ideas for how to turn the business around, and you hiring a nanny for Henry and going back to your job in California, I think it might be best for all concerned for me to move on, too."

He watched her remove the clothes from the washer and take them over to the drying rack.

He regarded her stoically. "I hired a *temporary* traveling nanny." *And only because you refused to go.*

Still keeping her back to him, she hung a string of seductively brief panties and bras up to dry. "And you'll find another one full-time, I'm sure. Probably before you get back from Europe."

Hart pushed the image of her clad in all that silk and lace from his mind. He waited until she had finished and turned back to him, before he asked, "So what are you saying?"

She went still. "That this has been great. I've loved my time with you—and with Henry. I'm still enjoying it immensely. I want us to be friends. And look back on this time fondly."

Aware this wasn't the first time in his life he'd gotten the verbal equivalent of a Dear John letter, he stared at her, waiting patiently for the rest. "But...?"

She shrugged and flashed a purposeful smile. "But nothing. You advised me to start living my life, and concentrate on the here and now." She reached for the hamper and tossed in a load of pastel colored pj's. "I've risen to the challenge. And you were right." She paused to measure the laundry detergent. "It did make a difference."

"Are you ruling out any future hookups?"

Maggie slammed the lid and pushed a few buttons. "I think we should play that by ear."

Irritated to find her running again, when they had so little time left together, he moved to trap her against the washer. "You have to be leaning one way or another."

She rested against the washer, arms folded in front of her. "Okay." She traded glances with him casually. "I'm leaning toward continuing whatever this is for a while."

He breathed a sigh of relief. A foot in the

door was all he needed. He'd made a whole lot more happen with a whole lot less. He stepped back slightly and conceded, "It has all happened pretty fast."

She nodded, still holding his gaze. "It has."

Her soft, suddenly compliant voice sent shivers over his skin, and blood rushing south.

He flashed her his most persuasive smile, hooked his arms around her waist and drew her in close. He feathered a string of kisses in her hair. Moved to the delicate shell of her ear. The elegant nape of her neck.

Figuring the best way to get her to see reason was to reframe her argument, he said, "And just because you and I have this incredible chemistry...that's no reason to make more of it than it is."

Her brow furrowed. She peered at him closely, as if not sure why he was suddenly agreeing with her. "Exactly."

Still trying to give her as much room as possible, lest she feel trapped again, Hart took her in his arms and made his own concessions. "Except I *want* to make more of it, Maggie," he told her quietly. She quivered and he stroked a hand through her hair.

"I want to know we're exclusive," he forced himself to go on in a rusty-sounding tone. "I want to know that even if we're living in different states, you'll be waiting for me when I return. That you'll make an effort to see me, and Henry, and the two of us will also make an effort to see you in return, no matter where you are living and working."

She paused, wet her lips, her blue eyes starting to shimmer. Yet as always, there was a part of her held back. Finally, she said, "That's generous."

He let out a low, rough laugh. Hating the fact they were running out of time to get everything set up before he left. "No it's not. I know what I am proposing is as self-involved as it gets. But here's the thing, Maggie," he told her urgently, looking deep into her eyes. "I can't imagine my life without you in it, anymore." He stopped and shook his head as his voice caught. "And I don't want to imagine it that way, either."

"Hart."

"Just give me a chance, Maggie. I'll stop pushing you to make too many changes too fast. But I can't slow down my feelings. And neither should you."

Maggie wanted to resist him. Wanted to keep everything on hold, but she could no more do that than she could deny how much she cared about him and wanted to keep him in her life.

So what if they weren't going to have everything she had ever dreamed of, everything she had ever wished for, she thought as they began to make slow, wonderful love. They had each other, this moment in time, and maybe someday in the distance, a future. It would have to be enough.

THE NEXT MORNING was as chaotic as Hart expected it to be. Henry'd had a good night's sleep and he was full of energy. Maggie and Hart had spent most of the night making hot, passionate love and were dragging. But it was a happy kind of dragging. One he wouldn't trade for the world. As she rushed around, getting ready for work, Maggie appeared to feel the same.

"More coffee?" he said, grinning while Henry raced back and forth between them.

Looking as thoroughly loved as he felt, Maggie groaned and pushed a hand through her still mussed hair. "Absolutely."

He was still spooning coffee into the filter when the phone rang.

Maggie answered. As she listened some of the color left her face. *"Already?"* she said. "No, I can't possibly. I have responsibilities in my current job. Yes, I understand. I'll try and be more flexible in the future." Maggie hung up the phone.

"Trouble?"

Maggie made a face. "The recruiter I'm

working with wanted me to drive to Dallas for an interview this afternoon."

She sure wasn't wasting any time. Hart forced himself to remain casual. "Is the job based in Dallas?"

Maggie nodded. "The best business analyst jobs available right now are for big companies in Dallas and Houston."

Cities that had big airports. Which meant direct, fast and easy flights to Los Angeles. Still… "You're only looking in-state?" He tried not to judge about that. Her family and friends were here. Hadn't he said he'd be understanding, that he wouldn't push?

"Yes." She smiled nonchalantly and went to get her earrings. "So, what's on your schedule today?" she asked, over her shoulder.

A lot, actually. Glad she'd brought it up, he said, "I'm taking Henry into San Antonio to get his photo taken and get the rush application for his passport filed. He has a pre-trip physical with a pediatrician after that. Then we're picking up his new nanny, K. C. Delaney, at the San Antonio airport."

Abruptly, Maggie looked at Hart as if he were missing something. He paused. "I guess I should get a guest room ready, too?"

Maggie made a face that indicated that wasn't it. "I can do that," she volunteered, all brisk professionalism once again.

Hart paused again, aware she seemed sort of...ambivalent. "You sure? You have a lot on your plate with the Randolph-Albertson wedding on Friday."

"It's no problem." Maggie ran a brush through her hair, gave Henry a quick hug goodbye, then rushed on out the door.

It was as if she wanted to stay extra busy, Hart thought. He knew how she felt. Anything to keep their minds off the goodbye that lay ahead. Temporary or not, it would still suck.

MAGGIE WANTED TO dislike K. C. Delaney. The nanny was taking over her place in Henry's life, at least on a practical level. So it was a relief, in a way, for her to meet the pretty, genial blonde. She was in her late thirties, of medium height and wore casual clothes that showcased her fit, tan physique.

Henry took to K.C. right away. He quickly showed her all seven of his small stuffed animals and his blanket. "Look, Kay," he said as he pushed each toy into her hands. "Look!"

To her credit, K.C. never tired of the game. By suppertime, she had Henry on her lap as often as he was on Hart's or Maggie's. Henry refused to let his new nanny rock him to sleep, however. He wanted Maggie for that. But otherwise, he took to her surprisingly well.

Hart was extremely relieved. Maggie told herself she was, too.

After Henry drifted off, the three grown-ups met in the kitchen to eat a dinner prepared by Hart. While they dined on pasta and salad, they went over the travel schedule. Maggie noted that K.C. was unfazed by the nine European countries they were going to visit in just fourteen days.

"It'll make it a lot easier to be on a private jet versus commercial," she observed.

Hart nodded, his expression grim. "He really hated the flights here. He cried the entire time."

K.C.'s expression turned gentle. "I'm not surprised that the poor little guy was upset. That was a lot for him to take in, in a very short period of time."

Maggie admired the other woman's compassion. But maybe that wasn't surprising given her regular job. "Hart mentioned that you also work as a pediatric nurse?"

K.C. nodded. "I only nanny when I need a break from the oncology ward. It can be intense sometimes. But getting out in the world, realizing how much life there is to be lived, helps me get back on track." She smiled brightly. "Plus, I love traveling. Love kids. Love being able to help. And doing this gives me chances to see places I wouldn't otherwise."

"Henry is very lucky to have you," Maggie said quietly. And so was Hart. "It's only been half a day, and he already adores you."

K.C. finished the last of her dinner. "He's obviously gotten very close to you, too. I thought you were his mommy."

Maggie felt like Henry's mommy.

That was the problem.

Once again, she had allowed herself to become swept up in the events around her. Once again, she was in way too deep.

"EVERYTHING OKAY?" HART asked from the office doorway, several hours later.

His sandy brown hair was clean and rumpled and a shadow of evening beard rimmed his handsome face. There was nothing special about his attire—in fact, the dark denim jeans, Western-cut blue chambray shirt and a pair of boots left over from his days on the ranch were completely ordinary. Yet he looked so thrillingly masculine and sexy, so much a Texas cowboy born and bred, standing there, Maggie felt her heart skip a beat.

She sighed inwardly. If only she could convince him to stay…

Yet, even now, he looked as restless and ready to move on, as ever.

A whisper of sadness swept through her, but Maggie forced herself to smile. She had said she could handle this long-distance thing, when it came to that, and she would. She stood and walked over to greet him with a brief hug and a light kiss on the cheek, then walked over to get the pages spitting out of the high-speed laser printer. "I'm trying to make sure everything's in order by the time your folks get back tomorrow morning."

Hart nodded, but his gaze said he knew it was more than that. He perched on the edge of her desk and watched her collate the papers she'd gathered so far. "Are you worried about Henry going to Europe with me?"

Not anymore. Maggie drew a bolstering

breath as she hit the Print command again. "No. I'm sure he'll be fine, with K.C. there."

He cleared his throat. "Speaking of K.C., will you be available in the morning to help us play a therapeutic game with Henry?" Hart paused, his gaze surveying everything about her, missing nothing. "We need your participation for it to really be effective," he finished softly.

Maggie knew she needed to be involved, if only for a little while longer. She nodded.

Hart smiled, then stood. "Anything I can do to help you here?"

Yes, Maggie thought wistfully, *please help me to not miss you so very much when you leave.* But knowing that was not possible, she shook her head. "The Randolph and Albertson families need itemized lists of all the expenses, thus far. It has to be emailed to them tonight."

If there was one thing Hart understood, it was the demands of the job. "Then I'll leave you to it." He left. Reluctantly.

She watched him go. Even more reluctantly.

By the time she crossed the breezeway to the main house, he was deep in another slew of work phone calls related to the tour.

Telling herself she was grateful for the distraction, she slipped upstairs, changed into her pajamas and climbed into bed alone. She fell asleep dreaming of Hart and the times they had made love and slept wrapped in each other's arms, while the new nanny and Henry slept just down the hall. And Hart labored on, downstairs.

The next morning there was yet another change. K.C. was first on the scene to get Henry up and dressed. Knowing it was best for Henry to get used to the new routine Maggie hung back.

"Daddy Har!" Henry yelled jubilantly, as Hart joined them, too; his low, masculine voice echoing in the upstairs hall.

Happy commotion followed. Maggie listened, her heart in her throat. Before she could do more than run a brush through her hair, the doorknob jiggled. Henry barreled in, a zebra tucked under one arm, a hippopotamus in the other, his daddy right behind him. Clearly, he was a toddler on a mission. "Mommy! Morning."

For once, she didn't bother to correct him on the name. She was so happy to see him, she hunkered down to face him and gathered him close. "Good morning, Henry."

Beaming, he hugged her back. "Breakfas'!" he said.

Hart lingered in the doorway. No pajamas this morning. He was dressed in boots, jeans and an expensive black-knit shirt that nicely delineated his broad shoulders and muscular abs. Just seeing him standing there, she felt incredibly safe. Incredibly wanted.

Incredibly aroused.

He flashed a sexy smile. "K.C. is making blueberry pancakes," he said, his gaze making her think he, too, was remembering the intimacy of their past mornings.

Dear heaven, she wanted him.

Now.

And it wasn't going to happen.

Not with his parents on the way, and a nanny downstairs, and Henry in her closet, emerging with a sneaker in one hand and a thin strappy evening sandal in another.

Laughter erupted from deep inside Hart's chest, even though he still looked like he wanted her. Here. Now.

"Breakfast?" he said, finally.

Maggie pushed the frog from her throat. Smiled. "Sounds great."

"Cakes!" Henry yelled, dropping the shoes and reclaiming his stuffed animals, then waving them high in the air.

Maggie shook her head at him affectionately, not sure whether she was going to laugh or cry, just realizing she was on the verge of both. Damn, she was going to miss both these guys. So badly.

Seeming to realize Maggie needed a moment

to pull herself together, Hart scooped his son—who had already pivoted back in the direction of her closet—up into his arms. "Meet you in the kitchen?" he asked, his voice sounding unaccountably gravelly.

Were his eyes just a tad misty, too?

Maggie nodded. "As soon as I'm showered and dressed," she promised.

HART HAD EXPECTED the introduction of a nanny into Henry's life would change the dynamics of their living situation at the ranch. And it had. Maggie was already withdrawing every bit as much as K.C. was drawing close. Now the question was: How did he get her back? How did he stop the momentum in the wrong direction?

Hart thought about that all during breakfast and into the morning. He was still mulling over his options when they gathered in the living room to address Henry's separation issues.

"We're going to play a game called Hello And

Goodbye," K.C. said. "It's to get Henry used to the idea that neither of you," K.C. paused to look at Hart and Maggie, "will be there for him every second of the day."

Which was what Henry had been used to, Hart knew. It was what he was used to, too. "So we're all going to say hello and greet Henry with a hug." The nanny demonstrated, then waited for Maggie and Hart to follow. Then, a few minutes later, they all said goodbye and hugged him and waved animatedly while they walked out the door.

Henry enjoyed being the star of the show.

Hart enjoyed just hanging out with Maggie and his son. He also appreciated K.C.'s expertise. He wanted to know his son was going to be okay without him. But the truth was, he didn't want Maggie to be okay without him, at least not long term. "Hart!" Startled, he looked up to see Maggie staring at him.

She shook her head in consternation. "It's your turn to say goodbye."

But he didn't want to say goodbye—not even for a couple of weeks. That was the problem. "Sorry," he muttered.

He forced himself to get his head back in the game.

And on they went. Repeating the scenario again and again. Until eventually, K.C. smiled and said, "Now for the final test. I want you to really leave this time. Both of you. Get in the car. Drive away. Wait fifteen minutes. And then come back."

"Both of us?" he asked. "At the same time?"

Henry was not used to that.

"It's important," K.C. affirmed.

Hart didn't want to go. Neither did Maggie. Yet they knew they had to prepare Henry for the inevitable. So they hugged him and waved animatedly and walked out the door. Waved animatedly all the way to the SUV and while they drove off.

When they got down the lane, Hart took a turn and started up the logging road. "This is killing me," Maggie said, her voice thick with tears.

Hart grimaced. "I hope he's not freaked out."

"One way to find out." She whipped out her cell phone. Dialed and hit the speaker phone. Seconds later, they heard K.C. pick up the ranch phone and say a cheerful hello. In the background was Henry's infectious laughter.

"Keep driving for another ten minutes," K.C. instructed. "I want Henry to know that when you leave him you will always come back."

Hart knew he would always be there for his son. But how could he make sure that Maggie would be, too?

Chapter Fourteen

"I admit it," Hart's mother said, after a cozy family dinner at the ranch that evening. "I am totally in love with my new grandson!"

"You're not the only one," Frank Sanders beamed.

Maggie was not surprised. Henry had warmed to his grandparents immediately, the confident, outgoing little boy such a contrast to the clinging, terrified child who had arrived at the ranch. Frank and Fiona had every reason to be proud of him, as did Hart. She was exceedingly proud of him, too.

Fiona turned to Maggie. "Thank you for all you've done for our son and grandson."

"We couldn't have managed without her," Hart added.

"I can see that," Frank said, with a wink.

Not wishing to get into that, for fear everyone would find out just how into Hart she was, Maggie escaped to the kitchen. In the foreground, she heard Hart giving his dad the business for teasing her. Luckily, K.C. had gone upstairs to give Henry a bath.

Hart's mother came in to get another glass of iced tea.

"I know you're head over heels for him, honey." Fiona gently touched her shoulder. "I can also see that you're struggling to deal with the fact he's leaving again."

Maggie turned toward the older woman. "But you aren't surprised."

"It's what he always does. We've accepted

that about our son." Fiona studied her carefully. "Did you think otherwise?"

Maggie admitted to herself that she had hoped something about being a dad would change Hart, make him long to be back home in Texas again. "I understand he has a job to do. Monica Day depends on him."

"It's good you're so empathetic. But don't be afraid to ask for what you need. That's important, too." Fiona hesitated. "With Hart leaving tomorrow evening, you're running out of time."

Maggie knew that. But how could she ask him to stay when she knew he had always wanted to be elsewhere? The last thing she wanted Hart to feel was backed into a corner.

They had an agreement. To take one day at a time, going forward. She was simply going to have to put her own needs aside, and honor it.

"IS IT OKAY if I rock Henry to sleep this evening?" Maggie asked, at bedtime.

Hart finished snapping Henry into his pajamas and handed his little boy over. "I'm sure he'd love that, wouldn't you, fella?"

Maggie knew she would.

Upstairs, they sank into the rocking chair. As she had so many other times, Maggie spread his blue blankie around his legs. Henry wanted to sit sideways across her lap, his head against her chest. He had a hard time situating all his animals just where he wanted, but finally he accomplished his mission and leaned against her contentedly.

"Sing, Mommy."

Because, she thought, Hart always sang. The only thing that came to mind was the corny wedding song she had once heard Hart sing to Henry. Holding him close, she began.

All too soon, Henry was fast asleep. Her heart breaking just a little, Maggie rose and put him in his crib.

MAGGIE PAUSED IN the doorway, Hart at her side. They stood together, staring down at the sleeping Henry, now snuggled contentedly in his crib.

Once again, it felt as if they were two parents, watching over their child. A lump in her throat, Maggie turned away and walked out into the hall. Hart followed, looking similarly affected. But not nearly as worried about their future as she was.

"Were you singing 'Going To The Chapel?'"

Maybe. "I don't know all the words, so I made up a few."

He pressed the tip of his nose to the tip of hers. "Cute."

He drew back, serious now, as he searched her eyes. "I have a favor to ask. I didn't get everything I needed done before I left. I'm headed to San Antonio. Want to ride along?"

"Now?" That's how he wanted to spend their last evening together? Driving to the city and running errands?

Hart shrugged. "Mom and Dad are already

in bed, asleep. So's Henry. K.C. said she would babysit."

Maggie glanced at her watch, still reluctant to waste their time on something so pedestrian. "We won't get there until after nine p.m."

Hart took her hand in his. "The place I have in mind is open twenty-four hours."

And in less than twenty-four hours he would be gone.

Why was she even hesitating? Hart and Henry were leaving in the morning to take a private jet to New York City. They'd be there long enough for Monica Day to do a round of publicity appearances and then go on to London after that.

This was probably her last chance to spend any quality time alone with Hart. She stood on tiptoe and kissed his jaw. "Just let me get my bag."

Hart had the SUV waiting in the drive when she came downstairs. En route to the city, they talked about the upcoming wedding, his parents' cruise and Henry's expanding vocabulary.

As darkness fell, they reached the outskirts of San Antonio.

Maggie expected Hart to stop at one of the discount department stores that kept late hours. Instead, he drove to downtown and came to a halt beneath the portico of a luxurious hotel along the Riverwalk. "What are we doing?"

Hart smiled mysteriously. "Taking care of some necessities." He took her hand and bypassed the front desk. Together, they stepped onto the elevator.

Maggie turned to him, her heart fluttering in her chest. "You have a room?"

His smile widened. "Not just a room." The presidential suite. Complete with a room service dinner and a bottle of champagne on ice, already waiting for them.

Maggie whirled to face him, wishing she'd known. She would have dressed up a little bit.

Still, she was secretly thrilled. "How and when did you manage this?"

He kissed the top of her head, the tip of her nose, the shell of her ear. "Today and very carefully."

Maggie tilted her head as he made his way down her neck, to the U of her collarbone. "Why?"

Hart straightened. He threaded his hands through her hair, looked deep into her eyes and confessed softly, "Because as much time as we've had together, Maggie, it hasn't been enough. Not nearly enough."

HART KNEW HE shouldn't be making love to Maggie tonight. He should be taking her out on the town, making up for all the real courting he hadn't had a chance to do. He should be using the time to persuade her to make more definite plans for their future. But when she looked at him the way she had been the last two days, as though she was all his one minute, but uncertain as hell the next, he also knew there was only one thing to do in the limited time they had before he left. And that was demonstrate his feelings in the most potent way he knew how.

"Ready for one of the most spectacular nights of your life?" He caught her beneath the knees, swung her up into his arms and headed for the bedroom.

Already looking deliciously tousled, Maggie teased, "Didn't we already do this?"

"The first day we met?" He set her down gently, aware that had been one of the most monumental days of his life, even though he hadn't known it at the time. He eased her out of her skirt and blouse. "Yes, as it happens, we did."

Maggie sighed contentedly and wreathed her arms about his shoulders. She waggled her brows suggestively. "Plus a couple of other times."

A couple of wildly sensual times.

Times during which he'd discovered just how much sex between two consenting adults could mean.

Lowering his head, he kissed her thoroughly, finally stopping long enough to confess, "Something about you brings out the caveman in me." He dropped his voice a register, pointed to his chest in true Neanderthal style. "Me, man." Then hers. "You. My woman."

She burst out laughing.

He joined in, aware it was a joke, and yet it was true.

She was his, even if she wouldn't quite admit it yet.

Their time together tonight would remedy that.

Drinking in the sweet, feminine fragrance of her skin, he lowered his head and kissed her, determined to make this last, to make their time together so real and amazing she would never want to be with anyone else again.

Her mouth pliant beneath his, she pressed

intimately against him, kissing him back just as ardently. Loving the way she responded to him, the way she trembled when they were about to make love, he put everything he had into the kiss, drawing back only long enough to reach behind her and unclasp her bra, and draw the fabric down her arms, baring her breasts. Need sprang up inside him as he cupped her breasts in his hands. Lifting the softness to his mouth, he stroked the nipples with the pads of his thumbs, laved them with his tongue.

"Hart…" Sighing softly, she clasped him to her.

"You're not ready yet." Not nearly ready.

Knees trembling, she looked down at him and moaned again. "Tell the rest of my body that."

Making this their most satisfying lovemaking yet meant not letting those soft helpless sounds she was making in the back of her throat speed things up. "Trust me," he whispered against the supple, silky heat of her skin.

He dropped to his knees and went lower still, kissing her through the sheer cloth. Hooking his fingers in the elastic waistband of her panties and dragging them down over her abdomen, the tops of her thighs.

She caught his head, tangling her fingers in his hair. "I do…." Already wet. So wet.

He planted a kiss in the triangle of dark curls. "Let me," he whispered.

Knowing exactly what she needed, he took her panties off the rest of the way.

"I don't think I can wait…" She hitched in a ragged breath as he cupped her bottom in his hands and ran his lips down the inside of her thighs.

His body throbbed. She was so beautiful and delicate. Aware he'd never needed anyone so urgently, or had more reason to proceed with care, he kissed her navel and the silky skin beneath. "We have all the time we need. Besides," he grinned, "you'll thank me later."

He felt her tremble again. Reveling in her responsiveness, he gently stroked her sensitive folds. Tucked a finger into her soft core, and found it damp, hot and tight. Still caressing her with his hands, finding the slick sensitive spot with his thumb, he didn't stop until she was fiercely aroused, her breasts tight peaks, her legs open even more.

"Let yourself go, Maggie." Needing to taste as well as touch, he found her with his lips and tongue. She gripped his shoulders hard. Let her head fall back, her breathing soft and ragged. Arching against him, she finally found the pleasure he sought to give her.

Enjoying how beautiful and ravished she looked, Hart clasped her to him, breathing in the scent of her, then moved slowly to his feet. He took her face in hand and kissed her again. "I love it when you tremble for me," he said. His hand dropped lower. He ached with wanting her, with the need to let go, too, even as she surrendered to him completely. His hand explored. "And open for me like this."

"Oh, God…Hart…" She rocked against him, close…so close…to coming all over again. "I want you inside me when I…"

Eager to please her, he undressed swiftly and joined her on the bed. She guided her hands around him. Suddenly, she wasn't the only one shivering with pent-up need. He was hard as a rock, throbbing, hot. She shifted and then he was inside her, filling her, creating a need only she could satisfy.

She wrapped her arms and legs around him.

Surrendering her heart and soul, just as he was giving his to her. Lips locked in a fierce primal kiss, she tightened her body around him, taking him deep, giving him everything he had ever wanted, everything he had ever needed. Showing him for the first time what it was to give and take without restraint. What it was to want to be with someone with every fiber of his being.

And love someone with every beat of his heart.

THE NEXT DAY, the time to leave the ranch came all too soon. And with it a surprise request. "Maggie, would you mind driving them to the San Antonio airport?"

Maggie turned to Hart's mother in surprise. "You're sure you don't want to go?"

Fiona shook her head. "Frank and I would feel better being here, since the Randolph-Albertson rehearsal dinner is this evening."

Frank agreed. "You've done all the work on this project so far. It's our turn to pitch in. Besides, Hart's departures have always been hard on Fiona and me, so we'd rather say our good-byes here."

Maggie had been thinking the same thing and had hoped to avoid any messy emotional scenes, but she couldn't refuse the Sanderses' request since they'd done so much for her. Still, she had to turn away from the hugs, and the sound of Fiona and Frank getting choked up as they wished the departing trio a good trip, to keep from bursting into tears herself.

Stay calm, Maggie advised herself, as she slid her sunglasses on and got behind the wheel of the SUV. It's only going to be a few weeks. Maybe a month. Or two. Then she'd go to Los Angeles and see them again.

Talk was sparse as they headed out.

Because it was his nap time, Henry fell asleep almost right away. When they reached the private airfield, the Learjet was waiting.

Henry was still asleep. Hart looked at Maggie. "Should we wake him?"

Maggie shook her head. If she had to say goodbye to him right now, she would lose it. "Let him sleep." A smile pasted on her face, she waited casually by the car while Hart carried the safety seat with his sleeping son onto the plane. K.C. followed. He returned to the car for the bags.

Suddenly she wasn't the only one with her heart on fire. He stared at her, with the same fiercely intent look he wore when they made love. "Get on the plane and come with us."

What? "That's crazy talk."

He grinned, all seductive male, bent on having his own way. "Is it?"

The impulsive part of her—the part that always jumped on everyone else's bandwagon—wanted desperately to say yes. However, the part of her that had been devastated by such impetuousness knew better.

Maggie drew an equalizing breath. "You have a nanny, Hart."

"It won't be the same without you."

He had to know it was killing her to say goodbye, even for a little while. She lifted a hand, abruptly feeling near tears. "Hart. Please…"

"What? Don't ask you to come along and share every single moment of some of the most incredible days of my life, as a dad, as a—?" He struggled, unable to find the right word that would explain what they were to each other.

"Lover?" she guessed.

His eyes darkened. Clearly, she thought, he did not want to be put on the spot. Nor did he think "lover" was the insult she took it to be. Because to her, they had always been much more than that to each other, even from the very start.

Aware this could easily blow up into something neither of them wanted, she tried another tact. "Look, even if I wanted to go, I don't have my passport."

He cast a look over his shoulder at the crew waving him aboard. Gave the one minute sign. "Is it at the ranch?" he demanded in the same take-no-prisoners voice she'd heard him use on the phone when talking business.

Finding herself unable to speak, Maggie nodded.

"Is it valid?"

Also yes.

He shrugged. "Then my dad can overnight it to New York. It'll be there before we leave the country."

And then what? Maggie wondered. Maybe if Hart'd said he loved her. Maybe if their plans had encompassed more than the occasional convenient hookup and visit, this would have made sense.

Maggie struggled to hold on to what reason she had left. "No, Hart. We have to say good-bye now."

He blew off the crew still trying to get him to board. "*Why?*"

Maggie took off her sunglasses so he could see into her eyes. "Because I've already done this before and I can't do it again," she said miserably. "I can't get so caught up in someone else's happiness that I suffer another doomed relationship."

His spine stiffened. "Is that what you think this is?" he asked, roughly.

"We don't love each other," she reminded him.

He blinked, an inscrutable expression coming over his handsome face. "You love Henry."

"Yes. I do."

His jaw set. "Just not me."

What could she say to that? Yes, I love you,

but you'll never love me, at least not the way I want and need you to love me, and I don't want to back you into a corner. Or make you feel trapped, or guilty, or any of the emotions I've spent the past two years grappling with. But how can I possibly tell you the God's honest truth—that I love you so much that I'm willing to let you go, even though it's killing me inside? Rather than have you look back with anything akin to the regret I've felt about every other impulsive action I've taken in my life.

Maggie inhaled sharply. "This doesn't have anything to do with how you and I feel about each other," she said, with a cool she couldn't begin to feel. "It has to do with common sense. And that dictates we stick to our original plan. You do your job, I do mine."

"Only one problem with that, Maggie." Anger flared in his dark brown eyes. "I don't need or want to take a break."

Maggie swallowed around the building ache in her throat. "You say that now. But a few months from now," she shook her head wearily, "when you start to get restless the way you always do, you may feel otherwise."

He looked at her, incredulous. "You think that little of me?"

Defiantly, Maggie held her ground. "We've both been engaged before because we got involved for all the wrong reasons."

"This isn't a mistake," he said gruffly.

"It is if you think our relationship won't survive a little break."

He caught her by the shoulders. "You're running away again." Hurt and resentment scored his low tone.

Blinking back tears, Maggie splayed her hands across his chest, holding him at bay. "Only because I know if we continue behaving so recklessly, we will both be hurt."

Hart stared at her as if she were a stranger. "A little too late for that, don't you think?" And on that word, he let her go, turned and boarded the plane without once looking back.

Chapter Fifteen

Two weeks later...

"Guess what I just heard via the Laramie, Texas, grapevine?" Her one-year-old son in her arms, Callie paused in the doorway of Maggie's office at the Double Knot ranch. "Gus and Nancy eloped last night. And they are crediting you and your talk to them about just having faith in each other and their relationship for prompting them to take the leap."

Maggie looked up from the job postings she had been reviewing online. She sat back in her chair. "Good for them. I'm really happy for them."

Callie stepped closer. "Ironic, isn't it?"

"Callie—" Maggie swallowed, her throat aching as much as her heart.

"How we intuitive types can always give advice, just not necessarily follow it ourselves."

As always, Maggie's twin knew when she was down, and these days, it seemed, Maggie was so far past merely depressed, it was ridiculous. "I'm getting out of my rut," she said defensively.

Just the way Hart had wanted.

Callie walked over to the play area and set baby Brian down amidst the toys. He babbled happily and immediately began to play with a toddler-sized set of interconnecting plastic building blocks that had been Henry's favorite.

As always, the memory of Hart's little boy sent an arrow of pain directly into the center of Maggie's heart.

"So what's it going to be?" Callie asked compassionately. "Are you going to apply for jobs in Dallas, Austin, or San Antonio?"

Maggie forced herself to be enthusiastic about the new direction her life was taking. "San Antonio. I want to be close enough to help you transition into your new job here."

Callie pulled up a chair. "Director of Marketing and Social Media." She reflected on her new title. "Has a nice ring to it, don't you think?"

Maggie nodded, happy about the new direction of her twin's life. Callie needed to put heartbreak behind her, every bit as much as Maggie did. "A very nice ring."

Callie continued to study Maggie, as usual not missing a trick. "Still haven't heard from him?"

Maggie took a deep breath, and through sheer force of will, pushed back the tears gathering behind her eyes. "Not a word."

Brian got up and brought a toy over to Maggie.

"When is the tour done?" Callie asked.

Maggie thanked her nephew for the "gift"

and gave him a hug. "They return to the United States tomorrow."

Bittersweet nostalgia for all the times she had spent with Henry filled Maggie's heart. She hadn't known she could hurt this much. Love this much. Miss this much.

Callie smiled as her son toddled back to his toys. "Is Hart going straight to California?"

Maggie released a quivering breath. "That was the plan, last I heard."

A thoughtful silence rebounded between them. Finally, Callie said, "I'm sorry. I really thought he would have called or written by now and apologized to you."

That would have been the gallant thing to do, had he really cared about her. Unfortunately, love had never entered into their calculations. They'd had passion. Friendship. Fun. They'd shared the parenting of Henry. But even that had been temporary. It wasn't Hart's fault Maggie had wanted more. She had known how committed he was to his job from the very beginning, that he planned to go back to the work and the travel. And that the only other accommodations he planned to make involved his newfound son.

If she wanted to help with that, great.

But if she needed time for herself, time apart from them, to figure things out, well then that was her problem. Not his. Or so he had said at the time.

Maggie shrugged and went back to reading the job listings. "It's for the best," she reiterated.

"Not when you walk around looking like you lost your best friend, it's not." Her sister silenced Maggie with a stern look, then paused to make sure she was really listening. "I lost the love of my life way too soon in circumstances I could not control. You have control over this."

Life was not as simple as her twin sometimes made it. "Do I?"

"Yes. You have a phone. You have a computer. You can call, text or email and say you're sorry."

Feeling like she would jump out of her skin if she sat at her desk any longer, Maggie stood. "But I'm not. We needed the time apart."

Callie stood, too. "And now you've had it. So what's changed? Are you over him?"

Heavens, no.

Brian turned and looked at them both with his big baby blue eyes.

"Have you ever felt about him the way you've felt about anyone else?" Callie challenged.

"You know I haven't." Maggie's voice was thick with tears.

Callie went to reclaim her son. "Then I only have one question."

The sight of her twin sister, cradling her baby boy, sent a fresh wave of pain coursing through Maggie's heart. *Not too long ago that was me and Henry, she thought.*

"What are you waiting for?"

"A sign," Maggie choked out. Something.

Anything. That said Hart might forgive her. Might give her time. Or better yet, somehow convince her they didn't need it.

"You've got a sign." Exasperated, Callie indicated Maggie's heart. "Right there. The only question is, are you going to finally stop being so darn stubborn, and heed it?"

A DAY LATER, K. C. Delaney stood in the aisle of the jet, during the last refueling stop of the trip, and gave Henry one last hug before handing him over to his daddy. "I'm going to miss you guys."

Hart gave the traveling nanny a familial one-armed hug. K.C. returned it briefly, hugging both Hart and Henry simultaneously.

Henry smiled back at her, content in the way he always was with K.C. Yet not upset to see her go. It was as if, young as he was, Hart's nineteen-month-old son knew K.C. was only destined to be in their lives for a short while. Still, they couldn't have handled the last two weeks without her. "We're going to miss you, too," he said.

Smitty walked over to shake Hart's hand. "It's been a pleasure. And thanks for the recommendation. It made all the difference."

"You've earned the promotion," Hart said.

Monica Day was next. She shoved her movie-star sunglasses to the top of her head. "I wanted to ask you if you were sure, but I already know the answer to that."

"I have to be there for Henry."

Monica smiled. "I understand. But if you ever change your mind and want to come back, either on my security detail or someone else's…"

"I'll give you a call," Hart promised.

The group got off the plane. Once inside the terminal, the entourage headed off in one direction; Henry and Hart, and their fully loaded luggage cart, in another. "Ready to go home?" he asked his little boy.

Henry took his thumb out of his mouth. He looked at Hart. And just as he had done multiple times every day the entire time they'd been overseas, said one word, plaintive, heart-wrenching and clear as could be. "Mommy," Henry said. "Wan' Mommy."

Images of Maggie filled Hart's head. Mornings. Late at night. In bed. In his arms...

Hart cuddled his son close. Out of the mouths of babes... "So do I, son. So do I."

MAGGIE ALMOST HAD her car loaded with her personal belongings when Fiona approached her with an unexpected request. Maggie furrowed her brow. She had a long trip ahead of her and she wanted to get started. "You need me to go up to Nature's Cathedral? Now?"

Fiona nodded urgently. "We have some new clients coming in, in thirty minutes. It would help us immensely if we at least had the wedding arbor set up."

Okay, Maggie had made sure to plan for every eventuality, which meant she had a lot of leeway. Still...she really wanted to get going! "And Frank can't do it?"

Fiona shook her head. "He went to town to pick up something essential. I know you're about to start a road trip, but you've got time, and this is important."

"Of course. I'll take care of it right away." Maggie got back in the car and headed up the old logging road. When she reached the top, there were two things she noticed immediately. First, the wedding arbor was already set up. So was the carpet they used for an aisle. On either side of it were two folding chairs instead of the usual dozen or so. Rather than facing the aisle, they were facing each other.

A motor sounded. Maggie turned, her heart in her throat, her emotions on the line. A Double Knot Wedding Ranch pickup crested the rise and rolled into the clearing. Hart cut the motor and emerged from the vehicle. He was alone. And headed right for her.

She used the time it took for him to cross the clearing to assess him. He looked good. Damned good. He wore an expensive dove-gray button-up shirt that nicely outlined his broad shoulders, muscular arms, taut pecs and abs. The dark gray slacks did equally nice things for his lower half. And though his boots were pure Texas, his short, sandy brown hair bore that perfect Hollywood cut required of a movie star's security chief. His ruggedly handsome face was clean shaven, his sable brown eyes intent. As he neared her, his lips curved into the determined, welcoming smile she loved so much.

The desire in his gaze made her tingle inside. "When did you get back?" she rasped.

He came closer still, seeming to catch his breath at the sight of her, too. Stopping just short of her, he affirmed, "Just now."

Her pulse pounded. Hope rose. Yet caution remained, too. "I gather you're the reason I was sent up here?"

He nodded. "I wanted to talk to you without interruption."

Ignoring the sudden wobbliness of her knees,

Maggie tried to figure out where all this was going. But first she had to know one thing. "How's Henry?"

Hart smiled and stared down at her with the quiet intensity she loved so much. "Rambunctious as ever."

The lump in her throat was back, as another wave of anxiety slid through her. "He weathered the trip okay?"

Hart's gaze drifted over her, as if he was memorizing every detail. "Other than asking for you repeatedly, he did just fine."

Tears blurred her eyes. "I missed him, too."

"So I told him as soon as we got back to the States, that we would find you, so you could see each other."

Was that all this was? Maggie wondered in shock, her spirits plummeting. A panacea for his adorable little boy? Hart's matter-of-fact expression gave no clue as to what he wanted, or even if he had missed her as much as she had missed him. The awkward silence between them stretched, emphasizing all that was at stake. Maggie ignored the tears pressing behind her eyes. "I missed Henry terribly, too," she choked out, "but if that's why you're here…"

"It's not." He wrapped a comforting arm about her waist. When she would have drawn away, he looked deep into her eyes, and held fast. "I understand you need more than a casual, long distance relationship with me, and an unofficial connection to my son. That you deserve a heck of a lot more. We all do."

Still trying not to read too much into this, Maggie released a quivering breath. "What are you saying?"

He tucked a strand of hair behind her ear, said softly, "First, what you already know. That Henry and I are a package deal. So," he inhaled deeply, "I need to know how you feel about becoming his mother. Legally."

It was part of what she wanted, Maggie knew, but was it enough? Could she settle for anything less than love? Should she walk away? Or was it time to go by what she'd felt whenever she was in Hart's arms, trust that he would eventually care as much about her as she did about him. Was it time, she wondered, to take that leap of faith?

SILENCE FELL. THIS wasn't going the way he had figured, Hart thought. Not that he ever seemed to have much of a cohesive plan when he was around Maggie McCabe. An odd fact, given his line of work relied on making detailed, ready-for-every-contingency-possible plans.

Aware he needed to reverse course—and soon—before he lost her completely, Hart shoved a hand through his hair. "That didn't come out the way I wanted," he said gruffly.

She lifted a delicate hand. "I understood you just fine," she whispered, moving away from him. The sunlight filtering down through the center of the trees illuminated her in a golden glow. When she swung around again to face him, her blue eyes were serious and searching. His heart ached at the vulnerability he saw in her face.

"But, before you go any further, I have something I want to say to you, too." She inhaled deeply and splayed a hand across her heart. "You were right about me from the very beginning, Hart. I have been running away for a very long time. And I ran hardest and fastest away from you." Regret colored her low tone.

He wrapped his arms around her. "Why?"

Maggie forged on, the words coming deep from her soul. "Because you made me feel things that scared me. I had put myself in a holding pattern for fear I'd make another, even bigger, mistake and I didn't want to come all the way back to life." Tears sparkled in her eyes, and she clasped his hand in hers. "You wouldn't rest until I did."

Maggie drew another deep breath, and continued. "I didn't want to feel like I could risk everything, never mind bank my entire happiness on someone else, for fear it would all fall apart again." She looked at him a long time, faith glimmering in her gaze. "However, you made me feel that I not only could—but that I'd never be happy unless I gave it that chance."

Wreathing her arms about his shoulders, she went up on tiptoe. "I love you, Hart Sanders. I love you enough to be with you, wherever, whenever, however. And," she cut him off with the impish touch of her index finger against his lips, "it won't be because I still have a case of raging baby fever and love your son as if he were already mine." She paused to let her meaning sink in, and once again, put everything on the line. "It will be," she finished emotionally, "because I can't imagine my life without you."

His heart swelled with love and a depth of satisfaction he'd never felt before. He gathered her close and kissed her soundly, letting everything he felt, everything he hoped for, everything he wanted to give her, flow into the caress. When they finally drew apart, he declared, "I love you, too. So much."

He hugged her tight, burying his face in the fragrant softness of her hair. They kissed again, even more passionately.

Satisfied all was going to work out with them after all, he gazed into her eyes and admitted gruffly, "I was going to tell you before I left."

She curled her hands over his biceps, holding him as if she never wanted to let him go. "Why didn't you?"

He shrugged, belatedly aware that was one of many mistakes he'd made with her. "Because I didn't want to say it and then leave. And I didn't want to leave and not say it, either."

"So you asked me to go to Europe with you instead," Maggie guessed.

Figuring if they were going to bare their souls, they might as well tell all, Hart sifted his hands through her hair and said, "The truth is, for the first time in my life, I didn't want to go. I wanted to stay right where I was, with you. But I couldn't. I'd made a commitment. I had to follow through on it. So, the next best thing would have been having you with us on the trip."

Her lips took on a rueful curve. "Only I refused to go."

"For understandable reasons, given how I issued the invitation at the very last minute."

It was Maggie's turn to shrug. "I didn't want to be something you'd regret. I didn't want to find out the hard way that all we were was a handy solution and a spur of the moment decision."

"I should have given you the time you asked for," he conceded.

She wrapped her arms around him, hugging him close. Tears spilled down her cheeks. "And I should have told you how I really felt then."

He ran his thumbs over her cheeks, rubbing away the free-flowing moisture. "Seems like we both made mistakes." His lips touched her temple, her cheek, the underside of her jaw.

"The question is," he asked, kissing her again, "where do we go from here?"

Delicate brows knitting, Maggie paused to regard him, then flashed a blissful smile, understanding him as well as ever. "I have a feeling you've given this some thought, too," she said quietly.

"I have. I want to marry you, Maggie. So if you'll have me," he proposed in a low, raspy voice that came from the very bottom of his soul.

Her McCabe-blue eyes promised everything he had ever wanted, everything he had ever dreamed possible. "You bet I will."

Epilogue

Eight months later...

Callie blocked the door to the train car where Maggie and her sisters were busy primping for the wedding about to take place in Nature's Cathedral. "Whoa there, fella," she told Hart. "You can't see the bride before the ceremony!"

Determined to steal at least one kiss before Maggie walked down the aisle to his side, Hart laid on the charm. "Then I'll close my eyes."

Callie inclined her head. "Nice try." Her voice was heavy with irony. "No."

Knowing a moment or two alone would probably ease Maggie as much as it would him, Hart continued affably, "Come on, now. There's no such thing as bad luck on your wedding day."

Callie's expression turned gentle, reminding Hart that Maggie's family knew him almost as well as Maggie did. As well as his folks knew Maggie. And Henry, well, Henry adored Maggie almost as much as Hart himself.

"She's not going to run away this time," she said quietly.

Damned right she wasn't, Hart thought. He'd taken plenty of steps to ensure that. Going as slow as Maggie needed to proceed. Living in separate apartments, starting consulting businesses for both of them in San Antonio—private security for him, business analysis for her—so they could control their own hours. And when they both were ready, he'd asked her parents for permission to marry her, proposed all over again.

Together, they'd gotten a ring. Planning a wedding ceremony had been easy—Callie had taken over most of the details. Finding a home they both loved, buying it, had been an even smoother process. Now all that was left was making it legal, honeymooning as a family in Hawaii—and moving into their new place.

"I know that," Hart said gruffly, not sure why he was suddenly the one with pre-wedding jitters. He just knew there was only one cure. He drew a slow, stabilizing breath. "I still need to see her."

Callie squinted. "*You're* not going to run away, are you?"

He scowled in return, his yearning to be with his bride growing as his patience fled. "Very funny." He pointed to his watch. "And time's a wastin'." Any minute now, the orchestra would be starting.

"Fine." Callie squared her shoulders. She gave him another militant glare. "But don't let anyone know I'm responsible for this."

Hart lifted both hands. "Hey. Discretion is my middle name."

She rolled her eyes. "And stay out of sight

until the coast is clear." Callie eased open the door to the compartment. "Bridesmaids! The photographer needs you all outside for photos right now! Maggie, you stay where you are!"

That quickly, all five of Maggie's sisters came out the door. They rushed past in a cloud of perfume and dazzling silk taffeta. His pulse racing, Hart waited until they passed, then moved up the steps and into the compartment.

Maggie was seated at the old-fashioned vanity reserved for the brides on their wedding day. His breath caught at the sheer beauty of her, and for a moment he could only stare, drinking her in, knowing he would remember this day forever. She looked perfect. Her long-sleeved dress fell to the floor in layers of figure-hugging white lace. Hopelessly feminine ruffles edged the V-neck, front and back, and fell from her waist, to further enhance the hem. Her dark brown hair was drawn back into an elegant knot at the nape of her neck. A wreath of flowers sat atop her head. She wore no jewelry yet, which was, of course, where he came in.

She put down her pearl earrings, caught his glance in the mirror, smiled, and swiveled to face him. As she shifted, he couldn't help but notice her shoes. The delicate high heels were meant to make his blood run wild and hot. They were also awful for sprinting anywhere, never mind through the woods.

As their eyes met, her expression said she knew what he was thinking. And understood.

Jitters fading, he began to relax. "No white cowgirl boots this time?" he asked with a grin.

"Nothing for a fast getaway, no." Their gazes met, held. "Although I did enjoy our encounter that day."

His body roared to life. He moved close enough to inhale the soft, womanly scent of her. He wound his fingers in hers, brought her to her feet. "You weren't the only one."

She sighed contentedly and leaned against

him. Savoring the closeness, he ran a hand down her spine. "Seems I'm always breaking rules where you are concerned."

Maggie wreathed her arms around his shoulders. "And vice versa." She stood on tiptoe and gave him a very tender, heartfelt kiss. As they drew apart, she paused to look deep into his eyes. "I love you, Hart Sanders."

His heart soared. "And I love you, Maggie McCabe." They grinned. Tenderness flowing through him, he kissed the inside of her wrist. "I have something for you." He reached into his pocket and withdrew a velvet box, similar to the one her engagement ring had come in.

Maggie glanced at him quizzically, then opened it, her fingers shaking slightly. Her gaze fell on the gold heart-shaped locket nestled on a bed of white satin. She bit her lip and opened the clasp, saw there was room for two pictures. Only a likeness of Henry was inside it.

Perplexed, Maggie glanced up at him. She

traced his jaw with her thumb. "No photo of you?"

He'd never seen her eyes look so blue. He kissed the center of her palm. "Actually, I thought we would save that for our next little miracle." Because these days he was restless for only one thing: more of what they had, right where they were.

His words resonated. Her face took on that maternal glow. "You want to have a baby?"

"We have been talking about expanding our family." And had been in complete agreement. The only question had been the timing. Maggie had insisted they wait until after Henry was completely settled, which he was, and they were married, which they were about to be.

A mixture of mischief and excitement gleamed in her eyes. "When would you like to get started on that?"

He pressed her body to his and drank in the scent of her hyacinth perfume. "Tonight?"

"I think that might be arranged," Maggie teased.

Hart savored the moment. They kissed again, even more tenderly.

"Now, for one last thing before we stroll down the aisle." Hart opened the door, stepped outside and signaled for the next surprise. His mom and dad handed Henry over. Hart carried the two-year-old inside. Like Hart, he was clad in a dark tuxedo, black silk tie and white shirt, as reminiscent of the Old West as Maggie's dress. He, too, had a boutonniere and shiny black cowboy boots.

"Mommy!" Henry yelled exuberantly, as happy to see her as always.

"Henry!" Maggie yelled back.

They both held out their arms. Henry ran to Maggie. Dramatically, the two embraced. Then, as had become their custom, both burst into a torrent of helpless giggles. Hart couldn't help but chuckle, too. "You two are a pair," he teased with all the love in his heart.

Maggie looked at him. "We're quite the family," she said softly.

"Yes, we are." Heart brimming, he went to join them.

* * * * *

MILLS & BOON®

Why shop at millsandboon.co.uk?

Each year, thousands of romance readers find their perfect read at millsandboon.co.uk. That's because we're passionate about bringing you the very best romantic fiction. Here are some of the advantages of shopping at www.millsandboon.co.uk:

* **Get new books first**—you'll be able to buy your favourite books one month before they hit the shops

* **Get exclusive discounts**—you'll also be able to buy our specially created monthly collections, with up to 50% off the RRP

* **Find your favourite authors**—latest news, interviews and new releases for all your favourite authors and series on our website, plus ideas for what to try next

* **Join in**—once you've bought your favourite books, don't forget to register with us to rate, review and join in the discussions

Visit **www.millsandboon.co.uk**
for all this and more today!

4/9/2014